STEWKEY

D. J. TAYLOR has written twelve novels, including *Trespass* (1998) and *Derby Day* (2011), both long-listed for the Man Booker Prize, and, most recently *Rock and Roll is Life: The True Story of the Helium Kids by One Who was There* (2018). His non-fiction includes *Orwell: The Life*, which won the 2003 Whitbread Prize for Biography, *The Prose Factory: Literary Life in England Since 1918* (2016) and *Lost Girls: Love, War and Literature 1939–1951* (2019). He lives in Norwich with his wife, the novelist Rachel Hore.

STEWKEY
BLUES

STORIES

D. J. TAYLOR

CROMER

PUBLISHED BY SALT PUBLISHING 2022

4 6 8 10 9 7 5 3

First published in Great Britain in 2022 by
Salt Publishing Ltd
12 Norwich Road, Cromer, Norfolk NR27 0AX United Kingdom

www.saltpublishing.com

Salt Publishing Limited Reg. No. 5293401

A CIP catalogue record for this book is available from the British Library

ISBN 978 1 78463 245 8 (Paperback edition)
ISBN 978 1 78463 246 5 (Electronic edition)

Typeset in Neacademia by Salt Publishing

Printed and bound in Great Britain by Clays Ltd, Elcograf S.p.A

'Ha' your fa got a dicker, bor?
'Yis, and he want a fule to ride him. Can yer come?'
Norfolk saying

In memory of Justin Barnard
1960–2021, who knew the territory

CONTENTS

STEWKEY BLUES

STEWKEY BLUES

THEY CAME UPON Stiffkey by accident, having tried and failed with Wells, Blakeney and Brancaster Staithe. From a car window all the North Norfolk villages looked the same. It had taken a week of barrelling back and forth along the A149 to establish that there was no pattern, and that only the fields of marram grass and the vast canopy of the sky were a constant. 'Looks nice,' Julia said as she reversed the Mini into a too-small space between two double-parked Land Rovers and a stricken 2CV that seemed to be held together with baler twine.

'It's pronounced *Stewkey*,' Nick said, who had a copy of *Ekwall's English Place Names* open on his lap and had volunteered similar information about Wymondham, Happisburgh and Great Hautbois.

'I bet it isn't really,' Julia chided. 'They just do it to annoy visitors.' In the middle distance, sunlight glinted off the mullioned window panes and the honey-coloured thatch and there were sandpipers bouncing in and out of the air currents. Even in mid-August there was no one about.

'I expect the coffee will be £3 here,' Nick said, who had paid £8.50 for a cheese baguette in Burnham Market two hours before. The coffee was £3.50. When they came back to the car half an hour later the 2CV had disappeared, but there was a sheet of Basildon Bond notepaper tucked under the windscreen wiper on which someone had written in elegant cursive script *A little courtesy to your fellow motorists would be appreciated.*

Julia twisted the note into a paper aeroplane and sent it spinning off to join the sandpipers. 'I just *love* this place,' she said, delightedly.

Fortunately they were the kind of people who could afford to live in Stiffkey, in both senses of the word. Julia's mother, Marjorie Devereux, summoned from Hertfordshire, plonked down £5,000 for the six-month rental without a murmur, pointed out that the damp course was defective and then drove off into the late-afternoon sun. Like the person who had left the note about parking, their new routines crept up on them by stealth. The CVs and the photographs of the people with whom Julia populated her poetry slams and her Arts Council-funded seminars – anxious-looking women with gypsy jewellery and pale boys with receding hair-lines – lay strewn around the sitting room. Nick took to conducting the Zoom conferences with the accountancy firms for whom he wrote marketing brochures and annual reports from the kitchen, laptop balanced on the pine table with its view of the distant sea. In the afternoons, when the gravel path to the beach became clogged with trippers and fat men in espadrilles with Mirror dinghies lashed to their car trailers, they went inland to Holt or Binham in search of second-hand bookshops and ruined priories. All this, Nick knew, smacked of ulterior motive. It was the same with the copies of the *Holt Advertiser*, the sea-horse pottery mugs and the sea-grass baskets with which Julia decorated the kitchen dresser, proof that in a world of tightly-demarcated boundaries and precise geographical margins, you had managed to go native. Here in North Norfolk the tourists were tolerated rather than encouraged. They lit fires up on the bird reserve and were run off by the wardens, and assumed that the baby seals left to sun themselves on Holkham beach were abandoned orphans. Nick had once seen a man in a Hawaiian shirt buy a dozen dressed lobsters at the Cley smokehouse without turning a hair.

Here in Stiffkey there were less expensive kinds of seafood. 'Try to get some Stewkey Blues,' Julia said, when he hazarded a trip to the fishmonger's. 'Granville says the locals love them.' He had genned up on enough coastal lore to know that Stewkey Blues were cockles, but Granville was a new name. Over the next few days, Julia's conversation thrummed with mention of him. 'Granville says we ought to get tickets for the Sea Fever festival at Wells . . . Granville says they have point-to-points at Fakenham . . . Granville says the best time to have dinner at the Red Lion is Wednesday night.' Like the scarlet buoys glimpsed at low-tide in Blakeney Harbour, he bobbed up when you least expected him. Forgetting to supply basic details of some phenomenon by which she was transfixed was one of Julia's oldest habits, in the same category as the Christmas cards she had drawn up by an artist friend each year, full of the same symmetrical holly sprigs and the same lumpy snow scenes. The cockles, meanwhile, which bulged suggestively against the rim of the giant jam jar in which they were supplied, were hard to swallow.

'They look like ogres' testicles,' he complained.

'Granville says it's because of the pigment,' Julia said, spearing one with a fork and up-ending it onto a slice of olive bread. That night it rained for the first time in a month – a colossal storm that punched up from the Hook of Holland and went rampaging off into Lincolnshire and whose after-effects demonstrated that Marjorie had been right about the damp-course.

Like the deluge, and the Tornado jets that came in low over the skyline at dawn, Granville was something unforeseen: not, as Nick had half-expected, the mournful exquisite in the three-piece suit who left for Norwich each morning in a Jaguar; nor, as he had occasionally supposed, the Wellington-booted ancient who could be seen pinning up details of church services on the parish notice board, but a slender, grey-haired 50-year-old with a lurcher, whom Nick found on the door-step on his way back from a walk picking samphire on the salt-marshes.

'Poor crop this year,' Granville said, tweaking one of the sprigs out of Nick's basket, crunching it under his front teeth and holding the stalk disgustedly between finger and thumb. 'Bit too woody for my taste.' He had one of those high, authoritative voices that brooked no dissent. The lurcher, staring loyally at him, grey flanks aquiver, could have stepped out of a painting by Landseer. 'Look here,' Granville said suddenly, as if they had been engaged upon some long, fruitless argument that only a single decisive gesture could satisfactorily wind up. 'I saw your wife the other day' – the assumption that Julia was Nick's wife seemed to define him in the same way as the gleam of fealty in the lurcher's eye – 'and we thought you might both like to look in for a drink tomorrow night.'

Who was 'we', Nick wondered. Granville and Julia? Granville and some as yet unspecified Mrs Granville? Granville and his mansion full of domestic staff? Unable to think of anything to say about the samphire, his non-marital status or the drink, he contented himself with a glance at the bruising sky. 'Looks like rain again.'

'I don't think so,' Granville said. He was already six or seven feet down the sandy drive. The lurcher plodded diligently at his heels. 'Come at seven,' he flung back over his shoulder.

Later, in the warmth of the still-fine evening, they sat out in the back garden where owls shrieked and swooped over the hedges and in the distance mysterious flashes of light broke over the mutinous sea. 'Granville came round to ask us over for a drink,' he volunteered.

'Oh yes? He said he might.' Julia, busy with the arrangements for a conference at the University of Nottingham, was deep in a poetry pamphlet called *Shriven by the Zodiac*.

'Do you know where he lives?'

'One of those newish houses down at the end of the green, I reckon. Do you think this is a good poem?' She screwed up her eyes against the fading light and tried an incomprehensible stanza or two. 'I was thinking of asking her to open the conference. Just before Arabella does her key-note.'

All the next afternoon, hard at work on a corporate finance brochure for Ernst &Young, Nick consoled himself by wondering about Granville's house. A baronial pile, at whose portal the lurcher drowsed in lonely splendour? A paving-slabbed exercise in neo-brutalism tucked under the sand dunes? In the room below Julia talked avidly to poets on her smartphone. She had big plans for *Shriven by the Zodiac* and was commissioning its author to lead an improv session. Coming down to brew coffee in the expensive percolator Julia had bought at Larners in Holt, he glimpsed the jam jar full of cockles, abandoned between the bread bin and a heap of tea towels advertising the Brancaster coastal trail. 'Naturally, I'm sympathetic,' he heard Julia saying into the smartphone, 'but I can't have Jessica going on about her womb any more.' Without quite knowing why, they found themselves dressing up for the evening call, putting on smartish shoes and, in Nick's case, ironing a shirt. 'This is like Cranford,' Julia said, suddenly adrift on an unfamiliar social tide and desperate to bring the boat back to shore.

Granville's house, reached a few minutes after seven ('He'll think it terribly rude if we turn up early,' Julia worried), confirmed that its owner, for all his punctiliousness, was a dark horse. It was a small, practically tumbledown cottage with a line of slates missing from the roof and a dead badger curled up on the raggedy lawn. Inside, the atmosphere was more reassuring. On his own turf, Granville's powerful tenor lost some of its twang. Offering drinks ('What's your poison?'), he might have been the Water Rat getting up a party in *The Wind in the Willows*. The drinks were all old-fashioned exotica – gin and vermouth, Campari and soda, angostura bitters. 'Never touch it myself,' Granville said when Nick asked for whisky, the implication being that no else should ever touch it either. From silver-edged photo frames balanced on the shelves of antique dressers, buck-teethed girls in one-piece bathing costumes stared sightlessly down. In the kitchen there were piles of old newspapers and cans of dog food. 'Really this place could do with a clean-up,' Granville conceded. It was Julia who saw the envelope addressed to 'The Hon. Granville Banstead' gleaming from a cushion. They were getting the measure of Granville now, Nick thought, sizing him up, pinning him down, the impoverished country gent in his rustic shack, where ancient silver winked from mouldy cupboards, and alumni magazines fell through the letter box onto a mat awash with pizza flyers. Going upstairs in search of the loo, he found himself looking for something that would undermine this stereotype – the wall of computers linked up to the Singapore futures market, the roomful of photocopiers awaiting despatch – but there was nothing to see: just an anchorite's bedroom with bare floorboards and a cracked mirror hung slantwise over the sink. They arranged to have lunch with Granville at a pub in Blakeney the following week.

'Isn't he *adorable?*' Julia said, in a way he had previously heard her speak of hamsters or friends' slapdash children, as they tripped over the slippery paving stones that had been sunk into Granville's garden, past the stinking badger.

'That bottle of vermouth must have been ten years old.' What did Granville do with his solitary evenings, Nick wondered. He had a vision of him brooding alcoholically over a meagre fire, or reading P. G. Wodehouse novels deep into the night.

'Tomorrow,' Julia said, who had admired the range of stout, sensible footwear on display by Granville's front door, 'I'm going to go into Holt and get myself a proper pair of boots.'

Autumn came in a rush. One moment the A149 was an unbroken conveyor belt of traffic; the next there were only farm trucks and hopper buses buzzing on to Hunstanton and Lynn. The fog, hanging over the salt marshes, could take hours to disappear. At dawn the sky bled extraordinary shades of cerise and magenta before settling down into an endless pale slate horizon, like the translucent toffee Nick had once seen on a trip to Hollywood being shaped into fake windows for stuntmen to jump through. 'I talked to mother about extending the lease,' Julia said one morning, the infinitesimal arching and un-arching of her fingers acknowledging a failure to discuss this in advance. Looking at her across the breakfast table – chilly now, despite the wall-heater – he registered some of the changes wrought upon her by three months on the east coast. They included a pair of lace-up leather half-boots from the Country Casuals store in Burnham Market and a cable-knit pullover from a shop in Wells that had cost all of £125. On the other hand, they were still sufficiently themselves to do imitations of Granville – the way he pronounced Edin-*borrow*, the mock-cockney intonation of 'me mother', his take on 'Hunstanton', which involved losing the second vowel altogether. 'I'll drive you to the station if you like,' Julia said, which was her way of apologising for talking to Mrs Devereux about the lease.

The autumn was Nick's busy time. It was then that the big professional services firms wanted copies of their annual reports and accounts – sober documents, heavy with the scent of corporate responsibility – to send to impressionable clients, when their senior partners were invited to address conferences held in Docklands amphitheatres. Twice, or sometimes three times a week he took the early train from Sheringham, changed at Norwich and spent the day in an office near Liverpool Street Station writing speeches about empowerment or polishing off case studies about companies whose treasury management systems had unaccountably failed them and whose lenders were about to foreclose. Outside the rain fell over Lothbury and Threadneedle Street and the familiar landmarks, looming out of the mist, looked odd and out of kilter. Who exactly was being empowered, he asked Mr Abrahams, the agency boss, and Mr Abrahams, who had laboured cynically in the Square Mile for thirty years, said

'Why, corporate communications specialists like ourselves, Nick.' Come the spring PricewaterhouseCoopers would probably want someone full-time, Mr Abrahams said, which was something Nick might like to think about.

But there were other things to think about back in London. One of them was the sub-let flat in Clapham with its ailing boiler and the language student tenants who had a habit of vanishing into the South Circular ether with their bills unpaid. Another was Julia, whose enthusiasm for her poets and performance artists dwindled with the November daylight. Coming back from Sheringham after one of his days out, as the gale blew in over the coast road and the taxi left a criss-cross of shattered tree-branches in its wake, he found her in the kitchen feasting off local produce: trout terrine on toast; smokehouse kippers; all the mysterious bounty of shore and stream. 'I thought you said you didn't like them,' he protested, eyeing the half-empty jar of cockles.

'It's an acquired taste,' Julia said, in the same decisive tone she had used that morning about the Clapham rent arrears. 'Granville's asked us to Fakenham Races this Sunday.'

There were plenty of acquired tastes here in North Norfolk, he thought, washing up in the empty kitchen as the wind swooped in under the door and the light bulbs danced in their shades: the espadrilled fat men with their Mirror dinghies; the head-scarved old gentlewomen on the beach who neglected to clear up after their dogs; a whole heap of complicated protocols just daring you to infringe them. The race course at Fakenham, a dozen miles away, turned up a subtle new demographic: deedy ancients putting each-way bets on the favourite; well-bred children in glistening cagoules; old ladies in Barbour jackets with hard, angular faces and tips acquired from confidential trainers. Granville, entertaining several of these people with the contents of a picnic hamper wedged into the rear-end of his mud-spattered jeep, was in his element: like Herne the Hunter, Nick thought, gliding through the forest surround and gathering up the fauna in his wake. 'Colder here than in Scotland,' he said. 'I was there the other week.'

'In Edin-*borrow*?' Nick asked, not able to stop himself, and felt, rather than saw, Granville's glint of disapproval. There was a particular horse, a pale grey mare, commended by Granville for the correctness of its gait, which sailed effortlessly over the jumps, while the animal Nick had backed came in seventh.

The trips to London were levelling off now. The senior partners of the accountancy firms had said what they wanted to say; empowerment was rife. Still, though, Mr Abrahams said, PricewaterhouseCoopers wanted him five days a week and were 'prepared to pay handsomely for the privilege.' Mr Abrahams liked these clichés. They reminded him of far-off days hobnobbing with the Cork Gully partners in their panelled luncheon rooms and writing press releases about the Big Bang. Knowing what Julia would say, he turned the offer down and, just to compound this sense of duty done, went off to Clapham on the tube, bled two of the radiators and helped one of the language students fill in her visa renewal form. Coming back to Stiffkey, an hour ahead of schedule, the warning text once again forestalled by the dodgy coastland signal, he found the house in darkness. A little vagrant music played softly in one of the upstairs rooms. Intrigued, he opened the front door and flicked on the light, but there was nothing to confound him: just a letter in Marjorie Devereux's crisp, italic hand together with more pizza flyers not yet retrieved from the mat, a mouse streaking off into the wainscot and the crazy shadows flung by coats and umbrellas.

Granville, hastening downstairs with white fingers doing up the buttons of his leather waistcoat, haphazard grey hair going in all directions, looked not exactly flummoxed but somehow cast adrift. 'Oh there you are,' he said from the third stair up, as if their meeting was the climax of some long and wearying search and now Nick could be returned to captivity. Nick had a terrible feeling that Granville was going to make one of his pronouncements about the weather, summon up some tropical typhoon that would sweep in through the open door and blow him off his feet in an instant. From above his head came the sound of anguished, pitter-pattering footsteps. 'Well, this is all very embarrassing,' Granville said, who did not seem particularly embarrassed. He had finished re-buttoning the waistcoat buttons now and was running his fingers over them as if they were the keys of some obscure musical instrument that might accompany him in song. Six feet away, Nick could still hear the mouse burrowing into the wainscoting as if its life depended on it. Following its trail, he moved off into the kitchen, where the remains of supper for two – plates, cutlery, fragments of bread and butter – still lay on the breakfast table. 'I should put that down,' Granville advised, seeing the cockle jar in his hand. Nick stared back at him. He could think of no insult worth administering, no physical gesture worth the effort. The jar spun in his fingers. For some reason he pulled off the lid, picked out one of the grey-blue globules that floated within and threw it hard at Granville's head. 'Fuck off, will you?' Granville cried. It was the most agitated Nick had ever seen him.

'No, you fuck off,' Nick said. The second cockle hit Granville square between the eyes.

'Nick, you'd better stop,' said Julia, appearing in the doorway in her dressing gown, knuckles up to her chin. Nick ignored her. All too soon his ammunition would be exhausted, but for the moment he was unexpectedly content. Granville skipped off back towards the staircase and he threw a third cockle and then a fourth, gripped by what might have been envy, or contempt, or some quite different emotion, as fathomless as the white waves that broke on the Stiffkey shore, half a mile beyond his outstretched arm.

CV

DANNY INGHAM IS born in 1958 in Lound Road on the Earlham estate. The house is small for the five of them – two sisters follow in quick succession – but they get along. Danny's dad works on the buses, driving the 85 along the long, threading highway of the Avenues to the old golf course on the city's edge where they are building the new university. His mother is a quiet, dark-haired woman who sits in the front room watching soaps on the black and white TV. The highlight of her day is the afternoon trip to Bunnett Square, a quarter of a mile away, to buy a copy of the local paper, the *Eastern Evening News*, and stock up at Davies's, the grocer on the corner.

Danny gets his first job aged 13, delivering newspapers for Sidney Lane. The sign in white letters on the blue shopfront says 'S. P. Lane.' Everyone knows that the 'P' stands for 'Peacock.' Sidney Lane is a small, bald man who lives in a flat over the premises and goes to Madeira for his holidays. The rounds stretch all over south-west Norwich, from the Earlham estate to the big houses on Christchurch Road. There is a fleet of bikes with outsize metal panniers kept in the yard for the delivery boys, but Danny likes to walk the route with the bag slung crossways over his shoulder. The people on the council estates take the *Mirror* and the *Sun*, whereas the people in the big houses on Christchurch prefer the *Telegraph* and *The Times*. Sidney Lane says he is a smart lad – people still say things like that then – and worth the £2 a week. Danny spends most of the money on records – *Ziggy Stardust and the Spiders from Mars; Slade Alive* – or presents for his sisters. The girls are shy and in awe of him, but they like the bags of candy bananas, the mini jars of sugared almonds and the faint cyanide scent that rises from their lids.

Delivering newspapers is harder than it looks. Some weeks Danny is spare boy, filling in for other lads who haven't shown. On unfamiliar routes the houses can be hard to find. Plus the round book changes when people go on holiday or leave the area. But Danny has a good memory and rarely makes a mistake. Pretty soon he has an afternoon round, too, out along the roads near Eaton Park and Northfields and is earning £3.50 a week. In one of these houses in Fairfax Road a boy Danny knows called Graham Cattermole, arguing with his mother, pushes her against the fridge so that she falls over, hits her head and dies. Meanwhile, decimal currency has come in and the big old copper pennies with Queen Victoria's head on them are giving way to tiny 1p pieces. Danny's dad, who has an eye for these things, keeps a couple of hundred in a plastic bag in the loft on the grounds that one day they will be worth good money to collectors.

Danny is in the fourth year at secondary school now, tall like his dad, with a chipped front tooth that he has never had fixed from when someone threw a satchel at him. His parents wanted him to go to C. N. S. or the Hewett, but somehow he ended up at the Bowthorpe in West Earlham, the worst school in Norwich, where most of the kids leave at 16. Mrs Marsden, the careers teacher, recommends a job at one of the boot and shoe factories, but Danny has a better idea. Mr Lane says he can help out at the shop, sort out the rounds in the morning and bag up the returns for collection next day by the delivery van. The pay will be £20 a week. Danny celebrates by tearing up his school blazer and drinking half a bottle of vodka from the Bunnett Square off-licence. It is the summer of 1973 and the newspapers' front pages have pictures of Mr Heath at the helm of his yacht, *Morning Cloud*. His mother's favourite TV programmes are *Coronation Street* and *Steptoe and Son*. His dad prefers the *Benny Hill Show*, which has big-breasted girls in their underwear scampering back and forth across the screen.

Somehow, working together in the shop, Danny and Mr Lane can't get along. They argue about getting the delivery bikes repaired, and whether to extend the rounds into West Earlham. Plus the work is exhausting – Danny has to be at the shop by 6 to sort the morning rounds and isn't supposed to leave until the afternoon boys are finished. In his mid-morning break he goes out into Bunnett Square and stares into the shop windows. There are several other premises on this side of the square: a chemist's; an old man who sells bicycle spares and ironmongery; Oelrich's the baker's; a betting shop and the Romany Rye pub. One November morning when Danny has just turned 17, Mr Lane finds him with his hand in the till, which is too big to be ignored. Danny, who knows that Mr Lane has been looking for an excuse to get rid of him, wishes he had left the £5 note untouched, but it is too late. Still, Mr Lane writes him a reference that says he is a *reliable young man who with the right kind of encouragement can make a valuable contribution to any organisation of which he is a part*. On the strength of this, Danny gets a job at the Rowntree Mackintosh factory in Chapelfield. The smell of cooking chocolate is one of the two smells that always hang over Norwich; the other is the reek of sulphur from the May

& Baker factory on the ringroad. Danny is put on the production line, in hair net and white coat, where his brief is to weed out duds, and is told he can eat anything he likes. The theory is that anyone who works at the factory will be sick of chocolate after a week, but Danny never tires of peppermint creams and Black Magic. In three months he has put on a stone. That summer there is a drought and the grass in Eaton Park turns brown for lack of moisture. His dad says he is worried about Danny's mum, who doesn't like to leave the house and some days barely moves from her chair in the front room. Danny's sister Alison, who goes to C. N. S., passes seven 'O' Levels, and says that she wants to stay on in the sixth form to study English, French and Mathematics.

Meanwhile, Lound Road is changing. The old people who have lived there since the estate was built are mostly gone now and the new families don't stay so long. There are more cars parked up on the narrow kerbs and it is less safe for children to play. When they first moved in all the neighbours were in and out of each other's houses, Danny's mum says. Danny thinks this is just the way older people talk. Chrissie, who lives in Thorpe in the north of the city, says her parents are just the same. Chrissie is a year younger than him and works at the Norwich Union Insurance Society. She is a pale, intense girl with bitten-down fingers, freckled skin and bright red hair twisted up in a slide. Chrissie likes Northern Soul music by Johnnie Guitar Watson and Wigan's Ovation and teaches him some of the dance moves. There is a pub five miles away in Sprowston that has Northern Soul nights and they go over there on the bus, walking home in the small hours through the dark streets. Some of the boys who come to dance can leap five feet high in the air. Once, jostling in the queue to get in, an angry kid waves a knuckleduster at them, but Danny faces him down.

Somehow Danny can't get on at the factory. The sweet, heavy scent of the chocolate boiling up in the vats makes him feel sick, and the job in the packing department, to which he graduates after a year, is deadly dull. Plus they are strict about time-keeping. Chrissie, who spends her working hours altering addresses in a giant box of index cards, says that Danny doesn't know when he is well off. In Bunnett Square the old man who sells ironmongery and bicycle spares closes down and is replaced by a boutique called Melanie's Modern Modes. Davies's the grocer starts selling oven-ready pizza and Ski yoghurt. Danny's dad is put on a different route, which takes him to Bungay, Southwold and the Suffolk market towns. His mum spends nearly all the day watching the TV now: the lunchtime news; children's shows; discussion programmes; anything. She has favourites among the presenters and complains when Angela Rippon isn't on. Danny's friend Keith, whose mother died when he was five, says it could be a whole lot worse. Danny and Keith know each other from way back at primary school. They go fishing at the UEA broad or the big trout lakes, staying out all night in tents pitched at the water's edge. When Keith says there is a vacancy at the butcher's where he works, Danny jumps at it. The butcher, Mr Daniels, is an old man with white hair and a sense of humour who calls his staff 'gents'. There are two other boys besides Danny and Keith. The job pays badly but you can buy meat at discount. Plus there are always people to talk to. Sometimes, when trade is slack, Mr Daniels tells them stories about the Arctic convoys he served on in the war, and being trapped below decks in a ship that had been holed beneath the waterline. Danny discovers that he quite likes working in the butcher's shop, heaving sides of beef into the freezer room or standing behind the counter in his blue and white pinstripe apron chopping up chicken pieces. He is smoking a cigarette outside the shop one morning in the spring of 1978 when Chrissie arrives to tell him she is pregnant.

In those days girls who get pregnant get married. It is as simple – or as complicated – as that. The wedding takes place at St Anne's church on Colman Road on a scorching day in June. Danny's sisters are bridesmaids, in bright yellow dresses from C&A. Alison will be going to Leeds University in the autumn to study Modern Languages. Melissa, two years younger, has a job as a dental nurse at the surgery in Earlham Road. Danny's dad says it is nice to see people making something of themselves, which Danny takes as a reproach. He gets drunk at the reception, which is held at the parish hall behind the church, and is sick in the taxi on their way to the hotel where they are spending their wedding night. Two weeks before Chrissie gives him a £20 note and tells him he has to be able to smile in the wedding photo. He takes the money to a private practice in one of the big houses on Newmarket Road and has the dentist fix his chipped tooth with a lump of amalgam. For a honeymoon they stay a week in a boarding house in Cromer that smells of fried bacon, and spend the time taking bus rides up and down the coast to Wells, Hunstanton and Burnham Overy Staithe, where Danny casts envious eyes on the anglers fishing for cod, skate and sea bass.

There is a plan to live with Chrissie's parents, but Danny and Chrissie's dad don't get on. Plus it is too far for his work. Instead they rent a flat in Cadge Road in West Earlham. Cadge Road is supposed to be the worst street in Norwich, but Danny doesn't mind. It is handy for the butcher's shop and the Five Ways pub where he and Keith talk about fishing. It is the winter where the Government are fighting the unions and the electricity goes off at unexpected times. The baby is born on Christmas Day in the Norfolk & Norwich Hospital, where there are sprigs of holly wound round the strip-lights and banks of Christmas cards on the bedside tables, and is christened Olivia Katherine Ingham, after the actress in *Grease*, which Chrissie has seen half a dozen times, and Danny's mum. Seeing her lying in the travelling cot that accompanies her back to Cadge Road, Danny is unexpectedly moved. He takes the baby out of the cot several times an hour to see if she is OK and gets up in the night to check on her. Keith, who has two of his own, says this is what kids do to you. Once again, things are changing. The university down the road in Colney is expanding, and the streets are full of students cycling in from their digs. Alison sends postcards from Leeds, says she enjoying herself and has a boyfriend called Hanif. Danny discovers that Chrissie, too, has plans. The spare room in the flat is converted into a nursery. Danny papers the walls and paints the ceiling, but it is Chrissie who suspends the mobile toys over the cot and installs the bright-ly-coloured fixtures. Seeing her at work, Danny wonders what has got into her and what the outcome will be. Meanwhile, Danny's dad says that his mum hasn't left the house in Lound Road for three months.

When Olivia is four months old, Chrissie says she has been thinking and that she and her friend Elaine are going into business together cleaning houses. Olivia can spend the day with her nan and grandad in Thorpe. Chrissie and Elaine call themselves THE CLEAN TEAM and work for women in the big houses on Newmarket Road, hoovering floors and polishing sideboards. The business is a success. With the first half-year's profit they buy a van with a picture of a woman banging out a carpet on the side. Just now Danny is planning to leave the butcher's, where trade is bad, the number of assistants has dwindled to three and Mr Daniels is thinking of retiring. Once, around this time, he reads a newspaper that says: PROSPECTIVE EMPLOYEES – WHAT ARE YOUR SKILLS? One thing Danny can do is drive. Even his dad, who taught him on one of the abandoned air bases out on the Norfolk flat, says he is a natural. He talks it over with Chrissie, and they decide that he will apply for a job at one of the mini-cab firms in the Prince of Wales Road. Chrissie has taken out her slide and has a new hair-style, bobbed and fluffed up at the front, like Lady Diana Spencer, who everyone says is going to marry Prince Charles.

Danny drives cabs for a decade and a half. He works for all the Norwich firms: 5-Star; Canary Cabs; Loyal Taxis; Gets-U-There. You rent your car for a certain amount a week; anything left over after the petrol is profit. Danny prefers regular customers: airport pick-ups; London-bound barristers who need taking to the station twice a week. There is an old lady who he drives down to Dorset each July to stay with her daughter. And every so often something comes along to break the routine. Once a man pays Danny £200 to ferry him all the way to Newcastle in the small hours: he turns out to be a criminal who has robbed a sub-post office in Dereham. Another time a scared girl with a baby wants to be taken to a women's refuge out in the country; Danny waives the fare. And then there are the celebrities: presenters from the local TV station; Norwich City footballers; actors who are on at the Theatre Royal. There is money to be made out of cabs, too: the students at the university want to be taken into Norwich to go to the nightclubs and brought back again afterwards. In a good week Danny can clear £250. Parked up in Bunnett Square waiting for a pick-up, he notices the changes. Sidney Lane has retired now, Mr and Mrs Davies have given up the corner shop and the Romany Rye, lavishly refurbished by the brewery, has become the Romany Beer House.

In the Romany Beer House, on the way back from visiting Danny's parents, on a Friday night in 1983, Danny and Chrissie have the worst argument they have ever had. It is over Danny's dead grandmother, Grandma Ingham, who leaves him £800 in her will. Danny spends his windfall on two new fishing-rods, a Norwich City season ticket and insuring his cab. Chrissie – white-faced and furious – tells him that the money could have been used for the deposit on a house, not to mention . . . And Danny knows that the thing not mentioned is that Olivia is getting on for five now. She has cropped red-blonde hair and skin so pale that you can see the veins beneath it, and nobody quite knows what is wrong with her. At the special pre-school in Bowthorpe where she goes three mornings a week, she sits on her own playing with a bag of toy bricks and ignores the other kids. When she talks, which is not much, only Chrissie can make sense of it. Meanwhile, Chrissie is expecting again. She dislikes the hot Norwich summer, when all the windows in Cadge Road are kept permanently open and you can hear people talking and watching TV. The baby is a boy and called Robert Angelo. Not long after he is born, Chrissie announces that she and Elaine are selling the cleaning business and starting a recruitment firm that will supply cleaners to hotels and offices. Plus there will be several thousand pounds freed up to move house.

The new house is in Eaton Village, detached and with a small garden where Bobby is put out in his pram on warm afternoons. From the start Danny is crazy about Bobby. He has him trying to kick footballs almost before he can walk, drives him around in a baby seat in the back of his minicab just for company. Always, if you ask Danny how he is, he will start telling you about Bobby. When he is seven months old they sit up late at night watching the Olympics on the TV, the swimmers' heads bobbing in and out of the water and Daley Thompson winning the decathlon. The recruitment consultancy does well, although Chrissie says Elaine isn't pulling her weight. Chrissie has taken to wearing crisp little business suits and doing her hair in a different way. Danny, who listens to her sometimes when she is talking on the phone to a client, is impressed but can see trouble ahead. Olivia goes to a special needs school where she is taught to cut circles out of a square of paper with blunt scissors and recite 'Baa baa black sheep.' The teachers say she is no trouble, as if, Danny thinks, this is the best anyone can expect. Olivia's class-mates have wide, gaping faces and are either listless or hyperactive. Danny doesn't mind admitting to Keith that they give him the creeps. There is a live concert on TV for the famine in Africa, and Danny, Chrissie, Elaine and Elaine's boyfriend Mark watch the whole twelve hours, barbecuing chicken and drinking beer, while the children play on the patio.

All of a sudden time is speeding on, moving faster than it used to. Danny has no idea where it goes. Alison marries her boyfriend Hanif and gets a job in marketing. Danny's dad takes early retirement from the bus company and spends his time in the betting shop, or going to the races at Yarmouth,

Fakenham and Newmarket. He still has the bag of pennies in the loft and says that one of these days he will clean up. Danny's mum has discovered *Neighbours*, with Kylie Minogue and Jason Donovan, but still doesn't like leaving the house. As for Bobby, one moment he is a red-faced toddler standing up in his playpen shouting 'Dad-dad-dad' at the top of his voice, and the next a silent, serious 10-year-old lining up with the other lads for Sunday-morning soccer games. Danny thinks watching Bobby play football is the greatest pleasure of his life. When the boy is through on goal, with only the keeper to beat, there is an indescribable feeling in his chest, as if there were yeast fermenting under his rib-cage. If Bobby's team – they are called Lakeford United – loses, he is inconsolable and mopes for days. Chrissie tells him not to take it so seriously. She does her paperwork on Sunday mornings and doesn't often get to the games. Once Danny gets into a shouting match with another man on the touchline who calls Bobby a cheat and the police are called. Danny's dad wins £2,000 on a six-horse accumulator and invites everyone he knows to a party in an Indian restaurant on the Prince of Wales Road that lasts eleven hours.

Danny and Keith don't see each other so often these days – Keith is living in Costessey with his second or maybe even his third wife – but they still manage to play snooker two or three times a month. On one of these evenings Keith says he has a proposition. Why don't the two of them start an angling shop? Actually, this is an old idea – they used to talk about it when they were fishing the UEA broad. Danny is enthused. He has visions of himself standing behind a counter flanked by pairs of wading boots and wicker baskets. Keith, who has just been made redundant from his last job, says there are plenty of vacant shops at the moment: all they need is a little capital. Danny and Chrissie spend a whole week arguing about the shop, which Chrissie says is a terrible idea. Olivia, who is sixteen now, big and fat and mysterious, sits on the sofa while they bicker, staring at a colouring book. Every so often Chrissie goes and puts an arm round her shoulder and strokes her hair. Chrissie has never liked Keith and says he is a bad influence. In the end Danny borrows £5,000 off Alison and this, together with Keith's redundancy money, is enough for a three-year lease on a shop in Mile Cross and the first consignment of stock.

The shop is called The Tackle Den and Danny is obsessed with it. He gets there early in the morning, long before opening time, and stands proudly in the window re-arranging the Angler's Club cards and positioning the beginners' rods in an arch over the door. Keith, too, is full of ideas. He wants them to do discount bait deals for competitions and get themselves photographed in *Fishing World* and the *Eastern Evening News*. But the shop is not a success. Fishing doesn't seem so popular as it used to be, and the angling clubs all have special arrangements with the big suppliers. Two years into the shop's existence, Bobby goes in late into a challenge, tumbles over on a hard winter pitch, breaks his leg in two places and has to have a metal plate inserted into the bone. It is so obviously not the other boy's fault that even Danny can't bring himself to protest. The injury takes six months to heal properly, and afterwards Bobby is nervous, shies away from tackles and likes to use his other, weaker foot. In Lound Road, half the houses are full of students and there is a Polish family, the Saluzinskis, living next door to Danny's parents. They are nice people, Danny's dad says, but keep themselves to themselves. Princess Diana dies in a car accident, and Danny remembers the time Chrissie had her hair cut that way.

There is something odd about Chrissie, Danny thinks. The recruitment agency is doing well, but she is worried about the kids. There is a care centre in Cringleford where Olivia goes three days a week, but Chrissie says most of the time they just sit watching television. Meanwhile, Bobby has taken to bunking off school – he says he doesn't but Danny knows better – and Chrissie thinks he has started smoking weed. Danny tries a man-to-man chat or two in the way his dad used to in the front room at Lound Road, but somehow it doesn't work with Bobby, who simply nods his head at whatever is said to him and looks shifty. Plus The Tackle Den is losing money. Sometimes a whole morning will pass and only half a dozen people come through the door for a nylon fishing line or half a pint of maggots. Keith says they need some new ideas, that they ought to go to anglers' conventions in Cambridgeshire and the Midlands, but the anglers' conventions are at weekends and Danny knows Chrissie doesn't like him being away. Chrissie is often away herself, seeing clients or going to trade fairs at distant hotels. She has a mobile phone which rings a dozen times an hour. When she is out, Danny and Olivia play Snap at the kitchen table. It takes Olivia ages to notice when the cards are identical, but Danny always lets her win.

When Bobby is 17 he is arrested, together with two other boys, for breaking into a house on North Park and stealing a wallet with £85 and two credit cards in it. After it has blown over – Bobby's solicitor manages to argue him out of the young offenders' institution and the court settles for two years' probation – Danny and Chrissie have a row that lasts three days. When it is finished, Chrissie says she is going to sell the house – the title deeds are in her name – and take the children to live in Spixworth with a man she met at a trade show at the Marriott Hotel. The man is called Roger – Danny has seen him once or twice – wears three-piece suits and has a handshake as clammy as one of the carp Danny lands at the UEA broad. Twenty years ago, Danny would have gone over to Spixworth and knocked out a couple of Roger's front teeth, but it is too late for that. Keith's accountant friend Doug has had a look at the books and says that the money Chrissie is prepared to pay him after the sale of the house will cover what the Tackle Den owes to the bank and the landlord and leave a few thousand over. The shop becomes vacant again, and Keith gets a job in security at one of the new nightclubs on Riverside.

There is talk of Danny staying with Melissa and her husband Tony – they have a spare room and wouldn't mind putting him up – but in the end he goes back to Lound Road. No one has slept in his old room since he moved out, and Danny is happy to pay for and hang some new wallpaper. Danny's mum is pleased to have him at home and gets up every morning to cook his breakfast. The Polish man next door – his name is Piotr – is a fisherman, and Danny sometimes talks to him when they meet in the street. One day Danny's dad says that Mr Vendulka, the Asian man who owns Sidney Lane's old shop in Bunnett Square, is looking for an assistant. To his surprise, Danny gets the job. There aren't so many people take newspapers these days, but Vendulkas employs five or six delivery boys and there is still the Menzies van to unload at 6.30 every morning. Sometimes, when one of the boys is off sick, Danny ends up doing the round himself.

The big houses in Christchurch Road still take *The Times* and the *Telegraph*, but the horse chestnut trees on the Avenues are nearly all dead or cut down. Saturdays, when Chrissie and Roger tend not to be at home, he goes over to Spixworth to see the kids. Olivia is always pleased to see him; Bobby smokes cigarettes in front of the TV. Danny's dad decides to cash in the bag of pennies, and doesn't seem to mind when the dealer only offers him £75. The newspaper Danny picks up in the shop every morning says there is war in Iraq. What with the money Chrissie gave him, there is £4,700 in his building society account. Danny, always good with his hands, thinks of putting it into a boot and shoe repair concession on the back of Norwich market.

LOST JOHNNY

HIS NAME WAS Jonathan Bennington-Smith, which was bad enough to begin with, although in mitigation ours was a school in which the patronyms ran to Crotch, Delavacquerie and Penhaligon-Pursley (there was even a boy called Simon Esterhazy-Mainwaring, although he lasted barely half a term), and his charisma, or notoriety – in those days the two qualities were indistinguishable – rested on his having in some mysterious way, at the age of about 17, 'let down' the headmaster's daughter Sally-Ann. This, it should be said, was the late 1970s and 'letting down' did not possess the range of undesirable imputations it has since acquired. It did not, to particularise, mean getting somebody pregnant. It did not mean delivering them in a supermarket trolley to A&E in the small hours, or abandoning them at a music festival while high on drugs. It may even have been something as innocuous as failing to turn up on time to a cinema queue, or omitting to return a borrowed copy of some set text. But it meant that Bennington-Smith, who was still at that point called Bennington-Smith, went through his last year at school with a kind of Byronic aura hanging over his not especially distinctive features. To add to this mystique, if that is what it was, was the fact that he played bass guitar in what was generally admitted to be the least competent of the school's three amateur rock bands.

All this may make it seem as if I was fascinated by Bennington-Smith, or at least thought him a person of consequence – someone to gossip with, say, in the school library on wet afternoons or drink coffee with in Just John's Delicatique, Norwich's solitary bohemian café. But this was not the case. My interest in him derived from the fact that Christopher Balfour, my bosom companion at the school since we had been nine-year-olds together in the first form, disliked him so much that the disliking became a kind of obsession, and that my mother, never known to take an interest in any of her children's acquaintances, and in spite of hardly knowing Bennington-Smith, and scarcely having the opportunity to observe him in action, regarded him rather in the way that a monarch might regard a promising young equerry. Each of these fixations - the one hard and unyielding, the other soft and indulgent - seemed to me so odd as to be worth investigating. Far more than the 'letting down' of Sally-Ann, whatever form it may have taken, or the playing bass for the Sapient Gophers, as they were known, it was these two sharply detached viewpoints that raised Bennington-Smith out of the ruck and gave him distinction. What made the situation even more unusual was that Bennington-Smith seemed not to understand that it had taken place. As far as I know, he never exchanged a word with Balfour, while his dealings with my mother were limited to nods of recognition when, as occasionally happened, they came upon each at the trackside on sports day or in the crowds of parents and their progeny who milled around the school playground after the annual prizegiving. He was like some formerly privileged hen, guilelessly wandering the farmyard, quite unaware that the farmer and his wife have already chosen him for the pot.

What I am trying to say, I suppose, is that even at this early stage - and my dealings with Bennington-Smith had several more decades to run, and may not even be done now

- I had some idea of the myths that accumulate around people and the elements of their personalities to which they adhere: myths of whose existence - this was clearly the case with Bennington-Smith - they themselves have no idea. But if I had no conception of how Bennington-Smith then regarded himself - all that came later - I knew precisely how he was regarded by other people and how that regarding had come about. Balfour's well-night fathomless dislike stemmed from an incident in early teen-dom, not even remembered by me, in which Bennington-Smith, taking to the stage at some low-level entertainment - the House Music Competition? Some charity concert? - was supposed to have exceeded the dimensions of the role allotted to him and 'shown off.' But whatever Bennington-Smith had done - and the event had taken place so far back in time that nobody except Balfour could recall it - was enough to damn him forever and con-textualise everything that he did, so that his appearance in a lunch queue, glancing uneasily at the trays of baked beans and over-grilled sausages, would have Balfour grit his teeth and mutter: 'Look at bloody Bennington-Smith making an exhibition of himself', even if, manifestly, no exhibition was being made. Curiously, my mother's high estimate of him seemed quite as arbitrary, plucked out of nothing, a frail seedling that had borne unexpectedly sturdy fruit. When I was ten or eleven, he had come, along with half the class, to a party of mine - these were the undiscriminating pre-teen days, when to associate with someone did not neces-sarily mean that you liked them - and somehow, out of the dozen or so boys present, my mother's eye had fallen on him. Afterwards washing up in the scullery, or returning the boxes of uneaten ice cream to the freezer, she had declared that he was 'a polite boy' who, additionally, had 'made things go with a swing.'

I myself doubted this. If anyone had made the party go with a swing it was a boy called Ashley Bushmill who, showing unexpected ventriloquial skills, had produced a surprisingly good impersonation of the Prime Minister, Mr Heath. But already the damage, if that is what it was, had been done. Generally speaking, my mother was too timid, too apathetic, to take an interest in my classmates in the way that my father did – asking which of them played for the rugby team, for example, or who had come first in the three-weekly order – but she made an exception of Bennington-Smith. On the occasion that the annual school photograph came into the house, having established that my own appearance was satisfactory, she would immediately set to work to pick out his face from the group of boys clustered around me. In my last summer term, attending a school art exhibition at which several of Bennington-Smith's paintings were displayed, she paid £10 for a smeary watercolour of the river Wensum at Pull's Ferry, which was hung in the dining room next to the print of Dürer's *Praying Hands* and an impressionistic reproduction of the Arc de Triomphe in furious little blobs of colour, which my parents had bought on their honeymoon. All three pictures looked absurd, but I could see, or thought I could see, how they chimed with the view that my mother took of the world, and that Bennington-Smith, who had 'made things go with a swing', was as important to her as an invitation to prayer or a glimpse of Parisian street life.

Naturally, once we had left school our relationships with each other changed. Boys who had spent seven years being certain kinds of people mutated almost on the instant into other kinds. The odd thing about these transformations was how they involved the same materials, the same personal characteristics. The script might alter, but the part was the same. Stolid and hitherto unexceptional boys who had done well in their exams became promising, but still stolid, undergraduates. Debonair but unintellectual charmers acquired jobs at the Norwich Union and became charming and debonair insurance clerks. To add to this confusion was the lack of basic information. People were moving off into the world and were difficult to follow. Sometimes they did not want to be followed, vanished off the face of the earth, were found working in pubs, or, in the case of a boy called Andy Hendrick, discovered selling knock-off jeans from a stall on the back of Norwich market. What had been homogeneous – the blue school uniform, the regulation hair-style, the common slang – was now bewilderingly diffuse. Six months before everybody - the law students, the insurance clerks, the pub factotums and even poor Andy Hendrick on the back of Norwich market – had been living under the same roof, eating the same terrible food and attending the same morning assemblies in Norwich Cathedral. Now, like a hundred soap bubbles, they were let loose on the wind.

To say that it took me years to track down Bennington-Smith would be an exaggeration, for there was no element of pursuit involved. Those were the days when information came upon you unexpectedly – the chance encounter on the tube train, the hand-written letter winging in out of the blue – rather than being served up hourly on an electronic plate. In Bennington-Smith's case this separation was made worse by its hint of mystery, which is to say that, despite seven years living cheek by jowl with him, I had no idea of the kind of person he was. All I had to go on were the projections of Balfour and my mother, neither of whom, experience suggested, were at all reliable. He was like a character in a half-remembered novel, drifting in and out of focus, and – you suspected – recalled for characteristics he probably did not possess. Around this time I received a copy of the school magazine. Traditionally this contained a page in which the careers of all those who had left the previous year were summarised in a couple of lines. Balfour's entry said that he had been a school prefect, head of Valpy House and secretary of the Debating Society. Of poor Andy Hendrick it stated merely that he had joined the school in 1971 and left it in 1978. Curiously, I approached this page of valediction – it appeared alongside the Lower School poetry supplement – with a sense of mounting excitement, anxious to see what the compiler had made of Bennington-Smith. If this was a boy whose existence seemed to consist of the myths projected on him by other people, then what would a formal survey of his teenage life look like? In the end, the resumé was almost as succinct as Andy Hendrick's. 'Jonathan Bennington-Smith (1970-78) played for the Second XV at rugby and was known for his musical accomplishments.' But even this, it seemed to me, was a travesty. No one had ever seen Bennington-Smith anywhere near a rugby pitch, and the musical accomplishments consisted of being just about able to play the descending bass-line of Free's 'All Right Now' at an end-of-term concert. Once again, he had slipped clear of the nets sent to pinion him and taken wing into clear blue sky.

It turned out that there were other people on Bennington-Smith's trail. One of them was Balfour who, the next time we met, after a withering recapitulation of the destinies being pursued by former member of the English set, said: 'I saw that bugger Bennington-Smith the other day.'

'Oh yes, what's he up to?'

'Apparently he was supposed to be re-taking two of his 'A' Levels at City College, but he said he couldn't be bothered.'

'So what's going to do next?'

'I don't know. I expect there'll be plenty of opportunities to make an exhibition of himself,' said Balfour, who was still cross at having failed to secure admission to University College, Oxford and could perhaps be allowed a little *schadenfreude*. 'Jesus,' Balfour said, who rarely blasphemed or raised his voice above the level of quiet irony, 'he was wearing a fucking *cloak*.'

'What colour was it?' For some reason I was entranced by this vision of Bennington-Smith skipping through whichever locale Balfour had seen him in wearing a cloak.

'White,' Balfour said, eagerly. 'Probably made out of a sheet. He looked like . . .' He paused for a moment and then, fixing on some of our generation's most potent figurative language, 'He looked like *Gandalf*.'

'What's it like at Leeds?' I asked, sensing that Balfour had said all he wanted to say about Bennington-Smith and that further enquiry would make him unhappy.

'It's OK,' Balfour conceded. 'Of course, they're all oiks'

As I have said – and it is a point that cannot be laboured too often in these considerations of time past – this was the age before instant information, when news of the things that had happened to people was not always readily to hand. Here in the twenty-first century, Bennington-Smith's career would have been a series of micro-progressions to which we would all – myself, Balfour, everyone else in our peer-group

– immediately have been party. As it was, the data slipped out by degrees, emerged in random fragments, took years to reconfigure into any kind of coherent shape, a process further confused by the fact that it was always possible to change horses in mid-stream. Thus, people who had started off studying Oriental Languages at provincial universities might be discovered, five years later, working as photocopier salesmen in the home counties. People who had sworn by the advantages of the solitary life and fixity of purpose would be found to have got married and fathered three children before they were 30. There was, it had to be allowed, a definite excitement in these disclosures, for they tended to fly in from nowhere. The veil of silence that hung over an individual life was suddenly twitched aside to reveal the triumphs, cataclysms or catastrophes that lay beneath.

In those days I used to read the *New Musical Express*, which came out on Thursdays and was printed in thick black ink that rubbed off on your fingers, and it was here, around about the time the Falklands War was coming to an end, that I first became aware of what Bennington-Smith had been up to in the four years since I had last set eyes on him. Like most news of this kind – news which, as it was not continuous, you approached from a standing start – it took me a few moments to appreciate the significance of the smudged photograph and the three or four paragraphs that followed, and to establish that the 'Lost Johnny' who had signed to Stiff Records was, in fact, the boy who five or six years ago had in some unspecific way 'let down' Sally-Ann the headmaster's daughter (now supposedly working in the costume department of the V&A), but the evidence was incontrovertible. It was also unsettling, if not humiliating then humbling. I might just by this stage have had a piece of journalism published in *The Spectator*, but Bennington-Smith had been signed to Stiff Records and had his photograph printed in the NME. This was not everything, but it was something, more unsettling still in that its effect was to confirm the sequestration of the world I had begun to inhabit, the world of Oxbridge colleges and cultured professions and innocuous entertainment. There were other lives being lived out there, out beyond the margins of the University Appointments Board, and Bennington-Smith – 'Lost Johnny' – was living one of them.

Six months later, at half past seven on a Thursday evening, I was sitting in the living room of the Pimlico flat in which I lived with a trainee stockbroker, an account executive from Saatchi's and a mysterious man who worked in import/export when the phone rang in the hall. It was Balfour. 'Stop whatever it is you're doing,' he instructed, 'and switch on BBC One. I'll ring you back in five.' Having left Leeds University with a II:1 and acquired a place at Guildhall Law School, Balfour was in better spirits these days. Somehow I had got out of the habit of watching *Top of the Pops*, but there it was, and there, indisputably, the moment I switched on, was Bennington-Smith, 'Lost Johnny', and a band of bubble-permed sidemen making their way through a number called 'Planet Earth is Calling You.' This, in case anyone has forgotten, was the era in popular music of what was known as New Romanticism, when brawny 20 year-olds who, five years ago, would have been wearing leather jackets and torn jeans, now arrayed themselves in cambric shirts, Turkish trousers and top-boots. As well as all these signature marks, Bennington-Smith was, additionally, brandishing a sword and had a three-cornered pirate's hat balanced on the top of his head. Like half a dozen other such songs currently in vogue, 'Planet Earth is Calling You' was upbeat, chirpy, and built around a nagging synthesiser pattern. At that point it would not have occurred to me to reflect that television does things to people, but I could see that this exposure, under the harsh light, before a yelling crowd (some of whose members were actually wearing scarves printed with the words LOST JOHNNY) had given his face a definition it had not previously possessed, that he was just as he had always been but somehow more so. All this had an instantaneous effect, by which I mean that in the two minutes it took to bring 'Planet Earth is Calling You' safely home to port, all the random impressions I had collected over the years were suddenly consolidated and given a fresh point of focus. It is not exaggerating to say that, in pulling on his Turkish trousers and balancing the pirate hat on his unruly hair, Bennington-Smith had become the person he was meant to be.

The same thought had occurred to Balfour. 'I gather it's already at Number 13,' he said, five minutes later. 'Most impressive.' With anyone else this change of tack might have given cause for comment. On the other hand, Balfour approved of material success. It would have been just the same if Bennington-Smith had been appointed junior partner in a City accountancy firm, or even managing director of a sewage plant.

'How's Law School?' I asked.

'Dreadfully dull. All the girls' boyfriends are other lawyers and they have terrible dinner parties where they talk about torts.' I knew that if the trainee lawyers hadn't talked shop at their dinner parties, Balfour would have been equally disapproving. 'Listen,' he said. 'According to this week's *Melody*

Maker, he's playing Dingwalls Dancehall in Camden Town next Thursday. We ought to go.'

'I thought you said you were too busy to come to London to see your friends?'

'Times change,' Balfour said enigmatically, 'and we change with them.' I had not seen him so excited since the day he claimed to have seen the former stroke of the school rowing eight coming out of a sexually transmitted diseases clinic.

If, on the one hand, our absorption in Bennington-Smith – 'Lost Johnny' – and this wholesale transformation of his prospects was unutterably bizarre (what was he to us? And what were we to him?), then, on the other, it was perfectly understandable. As teenagers we had in one way or another been brought up to regard life in what the Latin master, Mr Dickinson, would have called *sub specie aeternitatis*. On this scale of values, a pop star was slightly – no, a long way – below a minor poet or the crossword-compiler of *The Times*. At the same time, we came from a milieu in which what Bennington-Smith had done was altogether exceptional. The boys we knew became solicitors and chartered accountants. They might, if the cards fell against them, end up in supermarkets or selling knock-off jeans on the back of Norwich market, but they did not, by and large, appear on *Top of the Pops* brandishing a sword and wearing a pirate's hat. Around this time a writer called Andrew Sinclair published a novel called *Facts in the Case of E. A. Poe*. Sometimes with Balfour, on other occasions working independently, I found myself assembling facts in the case of J. Bennington-Smith. At that stage there were not many of them to hand, and what there was seemed tantalisingly obscure, only confirmed, or sometimes denied, when proper information became available. Nonetheless, even at this point the essential elements were plain to see. I do not think I am being unfair to say that Bennington-Smith's career in popular music was, if not a flash in the pan, then a short-term proposition. 'Planet Earth is Calling You' reached Number 9 in the singles chart and was followed by a second, minor hit. A third single sank without trace, while an album entitled *Lost Johnny's Lonesome Trail* spent a solitary week in the top 50. Subsequently, there was a legal case eventually settled out of court, in which three members of the backing band alleged that they, not Bennington-Smith, had composed the group's repertoire. Not long after this, Bennington-Smith was arrested in a pub in north London for possessing an imitation firearm and being under the influence of drugs and was briefly sectioned under the Mental Health Act.

Curiously, the person who took these revelations the hardest was Balfour. By now articled to a City law firm and 'walking out' (his description) with the daughter of a cabinet minister, Balfour had grown pompous. No, he had grown more pompous. 'He was dealt a perfectly good hand,' he complained, after we had read about the incident in the pub, 'and he should have played it better.' When I protested that life was not a game of bridge, that some people were simply not suited to the situations in which they found themselves, Balfour changed tack. 'He was always unreliable at school,' he said, substituting lack of capacity for a fundamental moral flaw. But there was more sorrow than rancour in his voice. Bennington-Smith, I divined, had in some obscure way let him down, failed to confirm the good opinion that Balfour had of him, and – an infinitely more serious matter – by means of this inadequacy called into question Balfour's good opinion of himself. Balfour liked the people around him to be successful. He did not read the novel I published around this time, but he displayed it on his bookshelf. When his girlfriend's father was sacked from the Cabinet, he broke off relations within a week. I could see that Bennington-Smith had let him down, just as he had let down Sally-Ann McClintock in the cinema queue, or wherever it had been. For myself, I was getting tired of Balfour and no longer accepted his invitations to watch Fulham play their home games around the corner from his flat. All the same, I was aware that, unlike Balfour, the collapse of Bennington-Smith's career did not make me any the less interested in him, either as an individual or as the repository of so much mythological sentiment. In fact, from this point onwards he became a kind of generational talisman, like a character in a novel by Anthony Powell, someone who without conscious effort on my part would continue to walk round metaphorical corners and recolonise my life when I least expected it.

Looking back on all this, at a time when some aspects of what happened seem inalienable, while others are even more open to doubt, I can see, however absurd this may seem, that my encounters with Bennington-Smith, once the two of us had left school, were almost exactly the same as my encounters with Iris Murdoch. In the course of twenty years I came across Murdoch four times. The first occasion was at a book-trade reception held at the Randolph Hotel in Oxford, when I became aware that the middle-aged couple standing next to me, and who resembled nothing so much as a couple of garden gnomes, were Dame Iris and her husband John Bayley. The second time was four years later, when. sitting in a chair outside a pub in St Martin's Lane, I watched as a small, dumpy woman with a helmet of dun-coloured hair and what looked like a Bloody Mary held level with her forehead came striding out of the interior and marched purposefully off into the summer twilight. The third time was six years after that, when I was introduced to her at a publisher's party (her first words were: 'Are you very left-wing?') The fourth time was a year or two before her death, when her mind had gone and she hung timorously onto Bayley's arm as they shuffled around the reception room at some gentlemen's club in Piccadilly.

Meanwhile, like Dame Iris and like Bennington-Smith, the world was moving on. The boys we had known at school were growing older, rushing on into their thirties, staring grimly into the abyss of the decades that lay ahead, drifting away into exotic quadrants where sometimes not even the school old-boys' magazine could fetch them back. People got married and had children, ascended to heights and descended to depths that no one could have predicted for them, and in one or two cases even died or, alternatively, vanished altogether, went abroad and never came back, found the other side of the world more to their taste than Norwich Cathedral or Mousehold Heath and never seemed to regret the transition. Balfour became a corporate lawyer with Clifford Chance in London and married a curious art-dealing woman with very short hair, a 180-degree social turn, which he justified with the remark that, really, he preferred bohemian girls. If I kept up with so few of them, it is because I lack skill both in keeping up and being kept up with. And yet Bennington-Smith, like Dame Iris, lingered there on the edge of memory, lingered in defiance of his elusiveness, far more real to me in his phantom shape than half a dozen people from those times with whom

I was in regular communication, or even Balfour, who was eventually forced to move to an artist's quarter in Maida Vale and name his first daughter Herculeana-Jade.

I should say immediately that I am not really concerned here with the first three of these four encounters with Bennington-Smith. Like the sighting of Dame Iris at the Oxford party, or abstracting the Bloody Mary, or child-like on John Bayley's arm, they were scarcely material. The first time was at the gig at Dingwalls Dancehall. This was an embarrassing evening on which Balfour, who had had too much to drink, attempted to finesse his way backstage after the show and was eventually up-ended in the street by a bouncer. The second time was in a Soho street, not far from Oxford Circus, when, in one of those odd moments so puzzling in life when one seems to have strayed onto a film set, I suddenly became aware that the man twenty yards behind me, head down against the breeze, was Bennington-Smith, and had just prepared the first of the sentences I was going to unleash on him only for a taxi to swoop down with such precision that it was as if the driver had planned his daily timetable in the certainty that it would coincide with his meeting Bennington-Smith in Wardour Street and carrying him away. The third time, possibly after the most loyal fan would have acknowledged his career to be over, was in a restaurant somewhere in South Kensington, when, just as I was leaving, I caught sight of him sitting in the corner of a crowded room with one of the women from Bananarama.

There are, of course, questions to be asked about these encounters, however immaterial they may have been. The important ones are these. What did Bennington-Smith look like? How did he seem? Had he recalibrated his personal manner to the environment in which he operated? The answers, I think, are that he looked wary, non-committal, keen on the privilege that his status allowed – the taxi swooping down on him in Wardour Street, Siobhan from Banarama on the table's further side – but all too conscious that it might soon be taken away. Later, when such things became available online, I watched several of his TV performances, and he looked not exactly half-hearted but oddly generic. He was a pop star doing what pop stars did to the level that was required for them to succeed.

But the fourth meeting was, I suppose, definitive. By this I mean that it established Bennington-Smith in my mind in a way that I have never been able to shake off. If the sighting in Wardour Street was like a moment on a film set – not a very glamorous moment, perhaps, but one in which reality seemed to be curling at the edges – then this final coming together was like the moment in a novel when a character, hitherto distinguished by infirmity of purpose, suddenly declares himself, shakes off one skin and acquires another. It was a dull winter day in the early 2000s, not long before Christmas, and, back in Norwich, I was walking past one of the department stores looking for a newsagent's that might sell me a copy of the *New Statesman*. On my computer screen that morning had arrived an email from Balfour saying that he was divorcing the art-dealing woman with the close-cropped hair and going off with someone called Henrietta Faversham. I saw Bennington-Smith long before he saw me and long before I recognised him. The delay in taking stock of and coming to terms with him undoubtedly lay in what he was wearing. For he was dressed from head to ankle in a firefighter's uniform – high-visibility jacket, thick canvas trousers, regulation helmet. He may even – at a distance of 15 years I am not certain about this – have been carrying a small axe in one hand. All this was impressive, and the power of the spectacle, as he stood there on the street corner, looking infinitely larger than the life that went on around him, had rubbed off on the other pedestrians, several of whom gave him nods or appreciative gestures as they passed by.

As I came up level with him I, too, nodded, but more elaborately than the others. I nodded like someone who means business, until Bennington-Smith swivelled on his big, canvas-covered legs to get a better look at me. Slowly – extraordinarily slowly, it seemed to me, while three or four more people went by and the taxis began to build up at the traffic lights thirty yards, away – recognition dawned.

'Weren't you at school?'

'I was.'

Two more pedestrians ambled past. They had already put up the Christmas decorations and the department store window on the other side of the road was bursting with holly and artificial snow.

'You were friends with that Balfour bloke. What's he up to now?'

'Works in the City. Some sort of lawyer.' There is nothing more banal than an eight-word summary of someone's career path.

There was something unnerving about the instinct that made Bennington-Smith fasten on the one person from his early life who might be said to have loathed him. Did he have any inkling of the way in which Balfour had regarded him? I was aware that, as the conversation went on, I was hard at work processing the information I had before: the sight of Bennington-Smith standing in the Norwich street; the firefighter's uniform; the mobile phone gripped tightly in one hand. All this, I could see, was a puzzle waiting to be solved. It did not seem odd to me that he had fetched up here in Norwich, where, it could reasonably be supposed, his parents still lived. He was seeking solace, I supposed, in a milieu that would appreciate what he had done earlier in his life and would happily forgive him for no longer being able to do it. At the same time there was something incongruous about the firefighter's get-up, not least the fact that it stopped at the ankles, after which a pair of white trainers took over. I stared at the trainers and then at Bennington-Smith.

'Did you . . .' – I struggled for a phrase anodyne enough to cover the change that had come over Bennington-Smith's life without embarrassing him – '. . . did you *retrain?*'

'I suppose you could call it that,' Bennington-Smith said. The mobile phone leapt in his hand and he glanced at the screen. 'You'll have to excuse me. Got to go.'

'Is there a fire?'

'Definitely hotting up,' Bennington-Smith said.

Until this point, entranced by the spectacle of Bennington-Smith in his firefighter's gear, and his trembling mobile phone, I had scarcely noticed the row of shops and other premises that had provided a backdrop for our conversation. One of them was a Mexican restaurant. Axe in hand – if indeed there was an axe – Bennington-Smith marched through the open door. By now I had grasped the essentials of this imposture. Any doubts as to what Bennington-Smith was up were finally dispelled by the fact that, as he passed through the Mexican restaurant's gleaming portals, he took a tiny, miniature fire-extinguisher out of his breast pocket and began spraying the contents to right and left. Fascinated to see what might happen, I followed him through the doorway.

The restaurant was small and badly lit, but Bennington-Smith, I could see, had already staked out his quarry. As at some pre-arranged signal, the group of women at the long table at the back of the room scrambled to their feet and, clamorously beckoned him towards them. They were Norwich girls, clerical girls in their twenties and thirties from one of the big offices in Surrey Street or St Stephens with wide, friendly faces and over-emphatic eyebrows. The girl whose birthday it was stood a little apart from the others, half bashful, half expectant. Expertly cutting her out of the pack, like a timber-wolf in pursuit of an ailing moose, Bennington-Smith whipped off his fireman's helmet, went down on one knee and presented it to her. There was something oddly touching about this gesture. If it was not exactly Sir Walter Raleigh abasing himself before the Virgin Queen, it had a definite air of grace and grandeur. From their vantage points around the room, other people – waiters, fellow-diners – looked more or less indulgently on. From somewhere above our heads, loud, abrasive music was starting up.

Leaving the helmet on the floor, Bennington-Smith got back to his feet and, gyrating slightly as he did so, and with a look of something very close to nonchalance on his face, began to undo the buttons of his tunic. From time to time he stopped what he was doing and ceremoniously anointed one of the women with a few drops of foam from his miniature fire-extinguisher. I left when he had got down to his canvas trousers and so did not discover just how far, as it were, the performance went. I am not sure, given the heightened set of circumstances in which we found ourselves – the shrieks of the more forward of the girls, the murmurs of the more self-conscious ones – that he knew I was there. Back on the street-corner the world seemed suddenly colder and less hospitable, although the noise spilling out of the restaurant as Bennington-Smith presumably completed his routine could still be heard by the people going by. I had already decided that I would not tell Balfour about this. Balfour, who worked for Clifford Chance and had gone off with a woman called Henrietta Faversham, would never know how Bennington-Smith – Lost Johnny – had comported himself in the Mexican restaurant. He would never see that look of exaltation on his face – that look of a man who is completely in control of the environment he so effortlessly bestrides, and he would never comprehend just how badly we – he and I and our class mates and even Sally-Ann, the headmaster's daughter he had so mysteriously let down – had underestimated him.

KID CHARLEMAGNE

'I SAW THAT programme about the Battle of Gettysburg last night,' Mr Sheldon said, one pale hand resting limply on the rim of the blue-grey metal till. He was a tall, thin, cadaverous man whose hobby was the American Civil war and who spent his leisure hours searching the TV schedules for occasional documentaries about General Sherman and Robert E. Lee.

'Oh yes,' Marcus said, non-committally. He was always non-committal with Mr Sheldon, on the grounds that a show of enthusiasm usually led to your being given some objectionable task to do: covering two dozen library books about wok cookery in plastic covers, say, or taking an armful of parcels to the post office three streets away. Mr Sheldon's pale hand was still resting on the till, like a stranded flatfish. 'Any good?'

'I think they under-played the attack on Culp's Hill,' Mr Sheldon said, with an immense, pained seriousness. The steam rising from the two mugs of coffee he had planted on the wooden surface next to the till rose dramatically to the ceiling like dragons' breath. Whatever was concealed in his other hand was making a brisk clicking noise. 'I don't suppose you know anything about these?'

It appeared that the previous day's haul of foreign currency had been even bigger than usual. There were two one-franc pieces, what might have been a rupee and even one of those African coins with a hole cut in the middle like a small copper doughnut. Marcus shook his head, seized the cup of coffee, which Mr Sheldon had made by sprinkling tablespoonfuls of powdered milk onto the surface and not bothering to stir them, and bore it off to a vantage point half way along the shop's L-shaped corridor. Here, trying to remember whether or not Felicity had said she would drop in that morning, he began to open a box of Penguins that had just arrived in the post. Five yards away, in the space between the sparsely-stocked children's section and the door to the staff lavatory, Mrs Sheldon, gaunt and predatory, sat typing invoices, her head bobbing over the keys like a shrike let loose on a game-keeper's gibbet.

'Oh Marcus,' she said, in her high, cracking voice. 'Could you not leave your coat on that chair? It's for the customers to sit on.'

Two months into his time at Sheldons, Marcus had already taken the measure of its proprietors. Mr Sheldon, though meek-mannered, could sometimes turn nasty. Mrs Sheldon, quarrelsome to a fault, was fundamentally good-hearted. The occasional rows they conducted on the staircase to the shop's lower level were of such magnitude that sometimes people would come in from the street to see what was going on.

It was about 10.15 now and still early. Outside in Bedford Street, a few shoppers tracked desultorily back and forth, slanting their heads against the fine February rain. Picking up his greatcoat from the chair, Marcus discovered that Mrs Sheldon had pinned a badge on it that said I READ BRUNA BOOKS beneath a picture of a rabbit. There was a sudden disturbance from the till and he saw that a rep had stolen in and was excitedly waving a catalogue under Mr Sheldon's nose. Mr Sheldon, who had an odd, impression-able side, was hopeless with the reps and could never resist their blandishments. The six fat copies of the Harvester Press edition of *The London Diaries of George Gissing* at £28.50 a throw that sat gathering dust in the window were a testimony to his failings in this line.

'Actually,' Mr Sheldon said, once he had disposed of the rep and dealt with an old gentleman who had got the front wheel of his bicycle tangled up in the shop's constricted doorway, 'there are one or two little jobs to do downstairs, if you wouldn't mind.'

Marcus stood back on his heels. 'One or two little jobs' could mean anything from a dozen orders to look up on the microfiche catalogue to ringing up the crazy woman in Attleborough. He was a small, discontented boy of 18 who was going to Oxford in the autumn – if, as his father often said, Mr Callaghan's government would leave him an Oxford to go to - and suspected that the months that lay ahead would be difficult to fill. Down in the airless basement at the tiny desk hemmed in by Sociology, New Age, Politics and Science Fiction, there were a dozen copies of a book about Victorian steam engines awaiting transfer to Norwich Central Library and a list of customers who needed to be telephoned and told that their books had arrived. Perhaps Felicity would come and see him in the afternoon. Who knew? Upstairs Mrs Sheldon was asking her husband in an accusing tone what had happened to the spindle of Book Token cards. Whatever Mr Sheldon said in return was lost in the whirr of the extractor fan starting up. Picking up the telephone receiver, he dialled the first number on the list, heard the click at the other end and, without waiting for the voice to answer, said in the most mock-deferential monotone he could muster: 'Good morning. This is Sheldons bookshop. The item you have ordered is now available for collection. Thank you so much.'

⚘

As the morning wore on and the routines of the shop fell into place, the regular customers began to arrive: Mr Weiss, the Prince's Street jeweller, who, showing his usual racial solidarity, bought a copy of the new Philip Roth; the trainee nurse who came in every other day to complain about the non-arrival of *Clinical Physiology Volume III*; the boy Marcus remembered from school who stood by the poetry shelf with one leg twisted around the other reading Ezra Pound a canto at a time. Of the eight customers he had telephoned, three had not been there and another three claimed not to have ordered the book he wanted them to collect in the first place. The rain grew heavier and lashed the plate-glass window. At 12.45 Mr Sheldon said he could go for lunch and he went out into the wet streets, which were full of clerks newly released from the banks on Gentleman's Walk and the Norwich Union Insurance Society, heading for the Lite-a-bite in the Royal Arcade. There was nobody much around. The Lite-a-bite had matted, fibrous carpeting like the husk of a coconut which, when trodden on, made the sound of leaves crunching on the forest floor. As he swung the rickety glass door back into place, Angie the red-haired waitress passed by with a tray of crockery.

'Get it on, Kid Charlemagne.'

But Marcus knew his Steely Dan albums. 'The people down the hall know who you are,' he threw back.

The décor of the Lite-a-bite was not easy on the eye. The

strip-lighting shone off the burnished chrome at peculiar angles and the black and white tiles that replaced the fibrous matting when you got closer to the counter were too highly polished. Felicity, brought here once at a time when several superior establishments were shut, had complained that it gave her a headache.

'Punishment of Luxury are on at St Andrew's Hall next week,' Angie said.

'Small fry,' Marcus told her. He was never quite sure where he stood with Angie, who half the time treated him as an indulgent elder sister might and the other half amused herself by bringing him things he hadn't ordered. Back at the shop, Mr Sheldon would be spending his own lunch hour browsing through a copy of *From Manassas to Appomattox*, while Mrs Sheldon stood vigilant at the till. When he returned from the Lite-a-Bite they would probably make him parcel up the text books that had been ordered by City College's Psychology Department or add up the credit-card counterfoils.

Some more people came in through the door, avid and wide-eyed, keen to see what the Lite-a-Bite had to offer. 'Marcus is an intelligent, thoughtful boy whose habitual cynicism is, I infer, affected rather than engrained,' the school's headmaster had written on his final report. A quarter of a mile away, up the hill beyond the market square, the City Hall clock struck the hour. Angie, slamming down the Welsh rarebit on the table-top beside him said, a bit more shyly than usual: 'I was in the audience once on *Top of the Pops*.'

He could not remember how Angie had found out that he was interested in music. 'How did you manage that?'

'My friend got us tickets. It was all right. We got to talk to Shakatak.'

She was a year older than him, or possibly two. He had once seen her, at a distance, in a pub on Guildhall Hill in a dress that was a size too small being bought what looked like Campari and sodas by a tough-looking character in a leather jacket.

The last piece of Welsh rarebit sat in his mouth like a piece of rubber. 'I'll see you,' he said, cautiously.

'Nothing here but history,' she countered, which would have been incomprehensible to anyone who had not recently listened to *The Royal Scam*.

Back in Bedford Street another parcel delivery had been stacked up under the main display table and Mrs Sheldon looked more gaunt and predatory than ever. It turned out that, in his absence, Mr Sheldon had apprehended a student from the UEA who was trying to steal one of the big art books, but had squandered this promising hand by ordering a dozen copies of a self-published book called *Prospecting the Norfolk Shore*. She was spoiling for a fight. Outside the rain still fell ceaselessly.

'I wonder,' Mr Sheldon said, in a mild way that always meant trouble, 'if you'd mind stock-taking Sociology. Magda' – Magda was Mrs Sheldon – 'said she thought they needed a really good going-over.'

Of all the tasks guaranteed to further depress a Wednesday afternoon in Bedford Street, stock-taking was by far the worst. Even worse than being sent to the cashier's department of the draper's shop on the corner in search of £5—worth of assorted change after the bank had closed.

'You can find those copies of *The Inner London Adolescent* and send them back to the publishers for a start' Mr Sheldon added, in the manner of one who offers an ice-cream to a fretful child.

Down in the basement the extractor fan had stopped working again, while whoever had been stationed there in his absence had occupied their time by starting to re-sort the Science Fiction shelves and giving up half-way through. Marcus crouched on the prickly carpet and began to put the books back. They had titles like *Tarnsman of Gor* and *The Stainless Steel Rat Gets Lucky* and their frontispieces showed men in space suits jogging along shiny astral highways. Just as he was slotting *Meltdown on Sub-planet Nine* back into the final space, he realised that the voice which had been in earnest conversation with Mr Sheldon a dozen feet above his head for the past half-minute was Felicity's.

There were people who said that here in 1979 there could not possibly be any women like Felicity left in the world. Well, those people were wrong, weren't they? She was a thin, spidery girl who wore costume jewellery, had her hair crimped down one side in a style he associated with the film actresses of the 1930s, wrote letters in a precise, blue-inked hand on expensive note paper that were full of exclamation marks, and signed herself *Yours most truly and affectionately Felicity Engledow.* She had also won a Brackenbury Scholarship to study Classics at Balliol College, Oxford, and his father, meeting her for the first time and not realising that there was anything between them, had registered his admiration with the single word 'Christ!'

'Mummy's still cross about that concert ticket,' Felicity said, as she came clumping down the wooden stairs in her stout, sensible shoes.

'I'm sorry to hear that,' he said. The concert ticket saga had been going on for so long that he could not remember the various incidents that brought it into being: what had gone wrong; who had failed to turn up; whether or not it was his fault. The details were as remote and unguessable as the thesis of *Modern Conservatism: A Guide*, which was staring at him from the Politics shelf. 'What brings you to town?' he asked. Felicity liked this kind of drawing-room cliché. She was quite capable of asking if anyone was up for tennis.

'I've been having lunch with Diana and Justine,' Felicity said, putting her handbag down on the table, behind which he had taken refuge. There was something sinister about the handbag, which was black and ominous and could easily have harboured a bomb. From upstairs came the sound of raised voices, and, as Felicity continued to tell him about the two terrifying gorgons she had been lunching with, he found himself trying to decipher what they were saying.

'Sophie really has behaved *incredibly badly*,' Felicity said, of some trivial misdemeanour newly chalked up to her younger sister's account. Marcus wondered if the women of Oxford would be like this, and decided that no woman could possibly aspire to such exacting states of hauteur and exaggeration. But then you took your female company where you could get it. You hung out with the people who allowed themselves to be hung out with and if that meant taking afternoon tea with Felicity Engledow twice a week, then hadn't some 18th century duke married his dairy maid?

By now the raised voices could be clearly identified as belonging to the Sheldons. All the other noises in the shop – the rasp of the extractor fan, which had mysteriously started up again, the patient shuffle of the customers' feet, the jangle of the doorbell – were secondary to this tumult. There was no way in which you could intervene in the Sheldons' rows. All you could do was to find a foxhole and wait for the bullets to stop flying.

'I really do feel . . .' Felicity began, craning her crimped head at the ceiling. She had strong views about many things: the Chelsea Flower Show; the leading articles in the *Daily Telegraph*; winter footwear. Just at this moment, one of the raised voices broke into a yell. There was a brief flurry of movement and a book – an actual book – which had presumably missed its target, came flying down the staircase, thumped against the carpet and then leapt up, like a live thing into the space between them.

It was too much for Felicity. Clearly some line – it might have been to do with him, or the environment in which he laboured, or some wider existential question of which he was only incidentally a part – had been crossed. She gave a little, stricken gulp, like a child who has swallowed too much orange squash, shot him a despairing but somehow contemptuous glance, retrieved her handbag and hurried back up the stairs. 'Flicka,' he said, into the newfound silence, but he knew it was no good. These things never were. Instead he picked up the book – it was a stout hardback edition of *The Diaries of Evelyn Waugh* – and set it down on the table.

Gradually the afternoon wore on. It was, everyone who had remained on the premises agreed, one of the Sheldons' best-ever performances. Several other books had been thrown and there was even some scuffling behind the till. Afterwards, flushed yet companionable, they went out for a cup of coffee, leaving him in charge of the shop. Later, in the pearl-grey light, propelled by some impulse he could not quite fathom, he found himself wandering down the Arcade again, where the boutiques and the coffee shops were closing for the day and picturesque old women with outsize carrier bags in their hands stood in doorways saying goodnight. The lights were still on at the Lite-a-Bite and he could see Angie's figure silhouetted against the wall of chrome and the row of empty display cabinets. The badge that said I READ BRUNA BOOKS was still pinned his lapel and he took it off and stowed it in the pocket of his coat. The conclave of picturesque old women stirred like troubled dreamers and began to move away. Angie, catching sight of him at last, made a deft, bobbing motion of her head that might have been meant to convey brusque dismissal, the sealing of a private contract, or something else altogether, and sent him silently on his way.

HEARTLAND

H ERE BENEATH THE humid pallor of a September
Sunday afternoon, there was something weird about the
Riverside. What was weird about it, Gary decided, skipping a
few paces on the balls of his trainered feet to keep up with Big
Kenny's marauding stride, what was indisputably weird, was
the smell. At two o'clock in the morning – their usual time
to be out and about in this particular locale – the Riverside
generally smelled of lager, vomit and gently diffusing cigarette
smoke. Right now, ten hours in advance of this nightly stake-
out in party-town, the mingled scents included cooking oil,
popcorn and something that Gary was pretty sure could be
identified as fresh air.

'Where we off to anyhow?' he demanded, as they swung
past the bowling alley and the patch of gum-flecked concrete
that abutted the multiplex.

'Boudicca's Chariot,' Kenny said, exchanging a curt professional nod with the two big black guys ranged squarely
outside the Queen of Iceni. Nearly all the clubs on Riverside
had local heritage names like Nelson's Porthole or the Kett
Saloon.

'New place, is it?' They were well past the Queen of Iceni
now, off into a debatable land of chi-chi hairdressing salons
and rabbi- hutch flats.

'Could call it a new place,' Big Kenny conceded.

'What's the name of the geezer who owns it?'

'Some Irish cunt,' Big Kenny said, whose grandparents

had arrived on the boat from Rosslare in 1935. 'Brannigan or some such.' By this time they had fetched up in a nondescript quadrant hemmed by boarded-up doors and spilled refuse sacks. 'Jesus. You have any idea where we fucking are?'

After a certain amount of time spent ringing random doorbells and accosting know-nothing passers-by, they ran Boudicca's Chariot to earth between a kebab shop and a row of lock-up garages. There was no one about except a lairy kid in a white tracksuit hunkered down in the doorway. Gary, who had been taking instructions from Big Kenny ever since they'd stashed the motor in the Rose Lane Car Park, grasped at the opportunity to reassert himself. 'Go on son,' he sternly counselled. 'Fuck off out of it.'

The kid – he was about 17, with two of those stupid disks plugged into his ear lobes that made you look like the representative of some benighted Amazonian tribe crawling out into the jungle clearing to gaze upon the great white chief in his helicopter – looked up inquiringly, wondered about venturing some smart remark, only to be silenced by the brazen symbols of Gary and Kenny's professional calling - the height, the muscle, the sleek Crombie coats – and slunk despairingly away. Cheered by this exercise of power, Gary sprang forward – Kenny was already ten feet ahead of him, racketing through the ghostly interior – over a tawdry expanse of cocoanut matting into the club's dark and unwelcoming heart.

❧

'You lads a team then?' Mr Brannigan wondered. He was a small, world-weary man for whom every aspect of their interview – the terse greeting at the door, the plod along trackless serpentine corridors, the ending up in the low-ceilinged, breeze-blocked cell with its single desk that was his office - was clearly far too much trouble.

'In a manner of speaking,' Gary agreed.

'How long?'

How long had he and Big Kenny been doing this? Christ, it was almost before they built the Riverside, back when the city's nightlife, such as it was, had boiled away in the confines of the Prince of Wales Road. While he was pondering these memories of bygone mayhem, Big Kenny said: 'Year Norwich went down from the Prem the first time.'

So it was 1995 then. Big Kenny's chronology was entirely football-related. If you asked him when his daughter was born he'd tell you it was the year Darren Huckerby signed. For the first time in their conversation Mr Brannigan expressed a mild interest.

'Remember a place called the Spinning Wheel?'

'Fucking horrible dump in Timberhill? Went there a couple of times . . . No offence,' Big Kenny added, suddenly divining why Mr Brannigan was so keen on remembering the Spinning Wheel.

'None taken.' For a moment Mr Brannigan looked more than ever like one of the gargoyles that hung over the west door of Norwich Cathedral. From far away, in some remote passage, they could hear the relentless drip of water. 'Now then, about your present duties. Eight till one on the doors. Bit of clearing up afterwards. Might have to shift the odd crate or two. We're not a big operation.'

'I ain't re-stocking no fucking fridges,' Big Kenny said, stung by the memory of previous humiliations in this line.

'No one's expecting you to restock the fucking fridge,' Mr

Brannigan said, as one leisure industry veteran to another. 'As for the money, it's eighty quid a night. No chatting up the birds on the bar and no charging taxis up to the club's account. Am I making myself clear?'

They nodded. The owners usually went off like this at the start. Then, if you were lucky, they started giving you bottles of Babycham or asking you to drive their wives to the airport.

'You see a lad hanging around outside when you come in?' Mr Brannigan demanded as they headed back along the corridors to the receding warmth of the September afternoon.

'Kid in a trackie and them fucking rings?'

'My boy, Shane,' Mr Brannigan said, in a tone that suggested he felt the same way as Gary about distended earlobes.

'Oh yeah? What's he do?' Gary tried to remember how kids of 17 occupied their time these days. 'City College? One of them new apprenticeships?'

'Sweet fuck all,' Mr Brannigan said. 'Helps out in the kitchen sometimes. You'll see him around, I daresay.' They were back at Boudicca's Chariot's shabby vestibule, with its peeling posters and unpacked crates. 'You lads take care now.'

It was a needless injunction. They were doormen. They always took care. Big Kenny leading, Gary bringing up the rear, calm and officious, big hands fending off the swinging doors as they bounced back, feet sinking into the over-moist carpet, they scrambled out into the edgy sunshine.

Back on Riverside, the breeze was coming in from across the Wensum, rattling the ships' masts and setting the window panes of the frail newbuild houses delicately aquiver.

'Let's go and have a drink,' Big Kenny said. 'Celebrate and all.'

'Celebrate what?'

'It's a fucking job, isn't it?'

'Last a fortnight in there you will,' Gary prophesied. 'Could see you eyeing up that cunt in his basement. You'll go and lob him one and we'll both be out on our arses. Like at the Saxon Spire.'

'Not gonna happen,' Big Kenny insisted. 'No way José. Not this time. Now, where we gonna go?'

And this, it had to be acknowledged, was a good question. Over the past 35 years - longer if you counted the hundreds of times they'd got in under-age - many a Norvicensian hostelry had enjoyed Gary and Big Kenny's sober patronage. The Volunteer in the Earlham Road. The Mitre, also in the Earlham Road. The Romany Rye, half a mile away on Bunnet Square. The Woodman - a long trip up to Catton but worth it once you got there. The University Arms at the end of South Park. Christ, half those pubs no longer existed, or if they did, had been turned into shops or veggie restaurants. In the end they settled on the Ten Bells in St Benedict's, which, it being a Sunday afternoon, was half-way deserted apart from a few teenagers for whom the downing of vodka shots was clearly a hugely exciting business.

'Where you living right now?' Gary asked, once the usual preliminaries had been dispensed with.

'Bullus Road, mate. Up the Bowthorpe.'

'Oh yeah. What's that like?' Bullus Road had been featured in the *Eastern Evening News* a couple of years back after an actual riot had taken place on the corner from which it debouched into Larkman Lane.

'They're fucking maniacs. You know what? Couple of weeks ago, after I'd gone to bed, the nutter next door only goes and jacks up my motor, takes the tyres off and tries to put them on some fucking Robin Reliant or something he's got dying on the pavement.'

'What did you do?'

'What did I do?' Big Kenny plucked a pickled onion out of the two-gallon jar on the counter and juggled it in his palm, like a vengeful fast bowler about to set off on his sprint to the crease. 'I jacked *his* car up and took them off again. Then I put a brick through his front door window. Nah, it's all right.'

'How's your Carole?' Gary wondered, keeping it low-key and casual, for you had to be careful when you asked how Carole was. Big Kenny gave a tiny, non-committal shake of his head.

'Actually, she's all right mate. Just now we got her – what are those things called you hang off the ceiling with all them wires and paper lanterns and such?'

'Mobiles?'

'Mobiles. Got her one of them. Loves it,' Big Kenny said.

❀

The reason you had to be careful asking Big Kenny how Carole was was that he might not like the question and you might not like the answer. Basically Carole's 17 – was it? – years on the planet had been a fucking disaster right from the star. All the stepping stones on this path to ruin were still fresh in Gary's head: the three days it took Carole's mum, Celeste, to give birth to her in the old Norfolk & Norwich Hospital in St Stephen's, with Big Kenny going spare in the corridor outside the delivery suite; the six incubator-bound months that followed, during which, to be frank, nobody really knew if the kid was alive or dead; her eventual discharge – she would have been about a year old by then; the semi-triumphant homecoming – Kenny had all his mates there on the doorstep to cheer her in – and installation in a nursery that looked like Emergency Ward Ten an hour after a bomb had gone off, full of pulleys and stretchers and winking lights and machines that beeped whenever you went near them. When she was six she started having fits – and not just your ordinary fits like the kids in the TV soaps who haven't yet been diagnosed with Tourette's or ADHT, but the proper screaming abdabs. Gary had been round there once, shooting the breeze with a cup of tea in his hand, when she kicked off and it was like some shell-shocked Tommy thinking he was back in the trenches. No, you didn't want to be there when Carole was away on one, or indeed on the more routine occasions when she was chewing up the ends of blankets or banging Tupperware boxes against her forehead, or chanting *erk-erk-erk* for half an hour at a stretch. Gary's domestic situation over in Costessey with Michaela and little Kayleigh was a picnic by comparison.

Except, that was, for those small-hours conversations.

Those small-hours conversations? Usually when he came home – this was at about three o'clock in the morning – stowed the Rover in the car port, checked on little Kayleigh under her magenta coverlet beneath the giant *Frozen* poster, examined his Twitter feed for any up-to-date news that @CanaryCitizen and @YellowandGreenArmy might have procured from their sources at Carrow Road and rolled silently into bed, he would find Michaela vigilant beside him asking things like: would he take her into the nursery tomorrow morning, or when was he going to fix the sodding drainpipe in the yard like he'd said he would. Last night, on the other hand, when he'd stumbled in, mazy and exhausted, shaking his head over the rumour that Toddy Cantwell might be signing for the Villa, it was to find her sitting bolt upright in bed with the light on, a cardigan draped around her ample shoulders and demanding: 'Do you believe in God?'

'Do I believe in what?'

Outside the window it was just your ordinary night in Costessey, which meant that there were sirens going off in the distance and the student rabble who rented the house three doors down were having one of their parties.

'Do you – *you*. Do you believe in God?'

It was, he supposed, a reasonable question. And in the course of a great many years spent tip-toeing into women's bedrooms when their occupants were supposed to be asleep he had been faced with enquiries that were a whole lot worse than this. The very worst had been 'Are you shagging my sister?' But not now, not in the small hours, not in Costessey, with the bump and judder of that crappy hip-hop nonsense bouncing away from three doors down.

'Jesus, Mickey. What sort of a question is that for three o'clock in the morning?'

'Well, you think about it, and come daylight you can tell me what you've decided.'

'All right then.'

In the end this eventuality was forestalled by their waking up to discover that little Kayleigh had been sick all over her magenta coverlet and the gerbil had died in the night (what was all that about? It had been fine when he'd filled up its water bottle the afternoon before). Still, as the day unfurled, as he negotiated the snarling traffic to drop Michaela off at the day nursery, as he slid and crashed around the shining leather sofa that Michaela had thought a suitable ornament to their cramped front room, browsing the sports pages of the *Eastern Daily Press*, as, finally, he stashed the Rover in the Riverside multi-storey and made his way through increasingly chilly streets to Boudicca's Chariot, he found the question leaching back into his consciousness. Did he believe in God? What was all that about? He had no objection to people going to church; and he knew that Michaela, always susceptible to the idea of spirit hands and ghostly presences, had started frequenting this place called the Big Hope Tabernacle on Sunday mornings. But asking you if you believed in God was a different thing. Did he believe in God? Was another, even bigger man up there somewhere looking down on him, seeing how he shaped up? Silently, disdainful yet perturbed, he passed on through the Chariot's garish vestibule to the company of Big Kenny, Mr Brannigan, weaselly Shane and the confines of the world he knew.

⁂

It was October now and he and Big Kenny were well established in their new routines. Clock-on at 7.30, uniform (the coat, the tie, the black Oxfords) in place, doors at eight. At half ten, if you were lucky, one of the girls from the bar - Julee, or Shirleen or the black one called Rita - would bring you tea in a Styrofoam cup. Close up at one, with a final shufti round the blighted alley at the back to make sure some tea leaf wasn't hanging about with an eye to the safe. Sometimes some mad girl would be found passed out in the toilets and you'd have to call an ambulance, and sometimes you'd see someone who was a bit too obviously dealing speed out of an imperfectly concealed plastic bag, but that was about it. Boudicca's Chariot was open five nights a week, Tuesday to Saturday, and oddly enough the worst night was Thursday. Thursday, for some reason, was when the tough boys came in on the train from Diss and Thetford and steamed through the place letting off fire extinguishers and jumping on tables. Or they did until they caught sight of Big Kenny, who had once – admittedly in his long-ago prime, when on duty outside the Nelson Hotel - chucked three Ipswich Town supporters one by one into the river.

Curiously, the most disagreeable thing about the Chariot was not the raiding parties from Diss or Thetford, or the lads off the estates peddling weed, or the white-faced girls throwing up in the khazi, but young Shane Brannigan, bastard cunt Shane, as Kenny, always handy with the prefixes, had christened him. What was it with those weaselly kids, Gary wondered. There had been half a dozen of them at school and several more at Lawrence & Scott Electromotors where he'd done - or hadn't done - his apprenticeship: under-sized nonentities with parchment skin, shifty expressions and a mouthful of sarky chat, always treading that fine line between keeping the company amused and taking it way too far, and Shane, advised the thirty years of bitter experience gained in such venues as the woodwork room of the Hewett School or the despatch desk of Goldcrest Taxis, where he'd filled in for a couple of years after leaving the engineering shop, was the worst yet. Shane, who when not making workshy cameos in the establishment's foyer with a steam cleaner, spent his time cadging drinks off the punters and hanging out at the bar. Another thing about Shane, too, was that he didn't seem to realise how far he was pushing his luck. 'Here come the Costessey boys,' he'd murmur as Gary and Big Kenny made their nightly appearance, which was not just disrespectful but plain wrong, seeing that Kenny lived off the Larkman, and Kenny would give him a not-quite jovial 'fuck off son' which Gary knew – again, that thirty years of experiencing bending his ear – meant not trouble exactly, but the promise of it glimpsed from afar, like the outriders of a gale shaking the tree tops half a mile away.

It was on the night that Kenny had added to his customary 'fuck off son' the words 'and I'm not telling you again' that the extraordinary thing happened. Well, not the extraordinary thing, perhaps, but the near-unprecedented thing. Usually, once the Chariot had closed down and the bar staff had been ushered into the waiting cabs, they'd saunter back along the Prince of Wales Road, past the crowds of milling kids and the volunteers from the rescue bus tending to the herberts who were being sick into gutters and the anxious coppers, for tea and toast in an after-hours joint Kenny knew about in Rose Lane where the taxi drivers and the girls from the clubs hung out. This particular evening, though, as soon as they were out into the street – there was a chill in the air and a big October moon glinting off the surface of the river – Kenny, with the air of powerful deliberation he brought to pools coupons and each-way bets, said: 'Come back to my place, mate?'

It was years since Gary had been asked back to Kenny's – five at least, the year Norwich got back in the Prem, back when he was living in Lakenham, which was weird, given how long they'd known each other, but that was Big Kenny for you. Gary knew better than to register any public surprise at this announcement.

'OK,' he said thoughtfully.

Following Big Kenny's car – a debased Vauxhall Astra which, like Homer's car in *The Simpsons*, gave the impression that if you rammed it up against a wall by mistake all the doors would instantly fall off – down the Earlham Road into the heartland, he found himself wondering how many times in the past 30 years he had driven back this way through the city, late at night. Two thousand times? Three thousand? There was no one much about, or rather, Gary hastily corrected himself, there *were* people about, but different kinds of people. Twenty years back there would have been the occasional night-shift worker ant, or a gang of students barrelling home, or even the old perv in the frogman's suit. Now there was a new kind of kerbside traffic: small-hours dog-walkers, even some nutcase jogger slipping between the traffic on his way to Earlham Park. Gary watched the Vauxhall reach the Fiveways roundabout, trailed it down Earlham Green Lane, took a right into the Larkman and then parked immediately behind it half-way along Bullus Road. Kenny, lumbering out of the driver's seat into the streetlamp's glare, looked even more substantial than usual. Christ, he looked about eight feet tall, like some superhero about to jump off into the sky. In three or four of the nearby houses there was a faint, or not so faint, whisper of music.

'Stay up late round here, do they?' Gary hazarded.

'Fucking nightmare,' Kenny agreed. 'Down here, mate.'

If it was five long years since Gary had seen the inside of any of Kenny's domiciles, then it had to be admitted that nothing much had changed. The big man took his clutter

– the football programmes, the DVDs, the creels and the split-cane fishing rods – with him wherever he went, like a turtle's shell. In the front room of the semi (there was another car in the drive, wheel-less and jacked up on brick plinths – where had that come from?) beneath muted pink light, Celeste, Big Kenny's wife of twenty years, lay fast asleep on a winded sofa. Carole, meanwhile – scrawny and wild-eyed - was parked in a kind of giant dentist's chair, rife with arm rests, back supports and ancillary clobber. 'All right?' Kenny said, not so much to Celeste or Carole as to the room at large, and Carole made the noise that Gary always associated with her, which was a high, mournful yelp, somewhere on the register towards scream, of *carc*, or maybe *cre-arc*, like a bull seal signalling to its mate on the flats at Winterton or Cart Gap. 'Jesus,' Kenny said, this time to the pile of debris at his feet. 'You want something to drink, darlin'?' and Carole began to rock from side to side, which presumably meant yes because Kenny then fetched her a beaker, which he placed reverently on one of the dentist's chair's platter-sized attachments. 'All right, darlin'?'

'*Carc*.' Hearing the noise, Celeste, whom Gary saw had put on *the fuck* of a lot of weight since he'd last seen her, quivered slightly – a kind of electrical jolt that went all the way round her body, from pudgy fingers to splayed, clod-hopping feet – came slowly awake and stared uncomprehendingly into the aromatic space that separated them.

'That you, Gal? What's he been and brought you round here for?'

'Can invite who I want round my house,' Kenny put in.

In the pink light, Gary thought that they all – Big Kenny, stooping over the dentist's chair, fat Celeste recumbent on the sofa, her torso covered in the pulverised residues of what looked half a dozen Cadbury's Chocolate Flakes, the parched, scrawny girl doing her tom-tom beat on the arm rest – looked slightly mad, and that he (he caught his reflection in big square mirror that loomed behind Celeste's corkscrew-curled head), looked slightly mad as well. There was a wedding picture of Kenny and Celeste on the wall next to the 45-degree-angled skein of ducks, which he remembered being taken because, in the capacity of Kenny's best man, he had been standing next to the photographer, shortly after he'd finished helping old Mrs Sullivan, Kenny's mum, with the washing up.

'How you been then?' Kenny was asking, one hand stroking Carole's rat-tail tresses, the other briskly administering juice ('*Carc*').

'I give her her tea. Tidied up' – Carole flung a plump hand around the piles of old newspapers, packets of incontinence pads and ancient VHS tapes with titles like *Yellow and Green Crusade* and *Canaries Golden Years* – 'and went to sleep. Why, what have you been up to?'

Kenny ignored her and addressed himself to Gary. 'Here,' he said. 'You remember that time the Millwall come in the club after the Norwich game?'

Garry nodded. He did indeed recall this long-ago incursion into the Pelican Lounge, which had ended with the brandishing of a fire extinguisher, the arrival of a riot van and a court summons on a charge of behaviour liable to cause a breach of the peace. 'You was really on one,' he said, admiringly.

'I was, wasn't I? What's that, darlin'?' ('*Carc*.')

Celeste had gone back to sleep. Her fingers scrabbled fitfully, as if she were trying to claw her way out of some lightless tunnel, far underground. Kenny had brought him here, Gary realised, so that he could indulge in one of his favourite hobbies, which was talking about the past. The old days, back at the end of the last century, when Kenny and Gary – the team - late twenties, built like brick shithouses, and primed not to take any crap – could be found six nights a week in the Prince of Wales Road, guarding the outsize portals of Mercy's or the Sugar Shaker, looking serious and telling people that they weren't coming in here dressed like that. They chatted a bit about this while Carole hiccoughed over her juice and Celeste snored until the moment came, as it always did, when Kenny shrugged, swivelled his eyes and loudly declared: 'Of course, it's all been – what is it? – *professionalised* these days.'

You could say that again, Gary thought. There were kids working the doors on Riverside with degrees in hospitality management, whereas in the old days all you'd needed was to weigh fourteen stone, put on a black overcoat and look handy.

'Different times,' he suggested.

'Different times,' Kenny echoed. Carole, too, looked as if she were about to fall asleep.

'Read to her sometimes,' Kenny volunteered, noting this development. 'Dunno if she takes it in but, well . . . You want a fucking Carlsberg?'

They had a fucking Carlsberg. Driving back through the grey-blue streets, from which even the dog-walkers and the joggers had disappeared, Gary thought hopelessly about the girl in the dentist's chair and Celeste asleep on the sofa and reckoned that he had a lot to be thankful for.

One of the things he had to be thankful for was the fact that by the time he'd got home Michaela was dead to the world. Because Michaela hadn't let up about the religious thing in the space of the last couple of weeks. No, the religious thing had got a whole lot worse. Item one in this catalogue of heightened spiritual awareness was the burial, in the back garden, ten days ago, of Damian the gerbil. He was just about to convey the cardboard box with its shrivelled, stiff-pawed corpse into the square foot of hollowed-out turf when Michaela, sober-toned and grim-faced, said: 'I think we ought to say a prayer.'

'Say a prayer! It's a gerbil, Mickey.'

'Probably on its way to a better world, for all you know. No, we ought to say a prayer.'

Whereupon little Kayleigh, only five years old but, as he fondly remembered, sharp as a tack, sensing the discomfort that pulsed between them and wanting to exploit it, piped up: 'I want us to say a prayer for Damian, so that when he goes to heaven Jesus will be nice to him.'

You couldn't say no to that. No way José. And so, heads bowed over the foot or so of dug-up lawn, self-conscious and intent, led by Michaela, they had said a prayer for Damian – something about him being much loved by little Kayleigh and taken from us far too soon. All of which confirmed Gary in his opinion that the best course of action would have been to chuck the fucking thing in the dustbin the moment it croaked.

And then, to add insult to injury, the other Sunday, Michaela had made him – had literally compelled him – to go to church with her. There were several quite serious objections Gary had about this. It wasn't that he had anything against religion. No indeed: Gary liked a carol at Christmas as much as the next man. No, his objections, apart from the loss of half his Sunday morning, were those of protocol and choreography. Gary wanted a church to be a church and a vicar to be, well, a vicar, whereas the Big Hope Tabernacle occupied a kind of tin-roofed shack halfway along the Bowthorpe Road, while its officiating cleric, Pastor Chesney – gruff-voiced and frighteningly hirsute – looked, to perfectly frank, like one of those blokes with a pile of the *Big Issue* under their elbows you saw shambling along Gentleman's Walk on Saturday mornings leading a dog on a string.

'What did you make of that then?' Michaela had demanded, as they marched out into the Bowthorpe Road, or rather as she marched and he trailed miserably behind her.

'Jesus, Mickey . . .' he'd begun and then fallen silent, because basically what were you supposed to make of anything these days, especially given the age you'd reached? You couldn't smoke a cigarette without wondering if this was the one that would fuck up your lungs for all time, and you couldn't stare enviously at the Range Rovers in the showroom out on the road to the airport without remembering that Greta Thunberg and her weevil mates were on your tail. Silent, thoughtful and with little Kayleigh - sprung from the children's corner at the service's close along with a multi-coloured crayon sketch of the Archangel Gabriel - glowing at his side, he allowed himself to be taken off home for Sunday brunch.

∞

On the other hand, one of the things Pastor Chesney had had to say in the course of his half-hour homily was certainly true: The afflicted shall find comfort where they least expect it. Now that, Gary thought, surveying the faces of the Chariot's non-executive staff as they sat round the bar the following Tuesday night, was bang on the money. Nobody, except for Gary, was supposed to know anything about Big Kenny's domestic travails, but somehow everybody did. More to the point, all of them – Rodney, who managed the bar, Julee, Shirleen and the black girl Rita – could be seen quietly extending sympathy, making Kenny cups of tea and asking him how he was all the time. And these, Gary reflected, were tough girls off the Mile Cross Estate and elsewhere, tough girls whose ancestral forebears he remembered from 30 years ago, stalking across zebra crossings without thought for the concertina'd traffic as they told their parrot-haired friends that they fucking hated Wednesdays or that that Ashley was a cunt. And they all were sitting round the bar, the girls with vodka-tonics, Gary and Kenny keeping it professional with Diet Cokes, waiting for their employer to emerge from his lair and tell them it was time to open up, and doing what they did at these times, which, basically, was to trade injurious gossip about Mr Brannigan, his dependents and his personal habits.

'Where's he live then?' Kenny asked, the tumbler of Diet Coke almost lost in his giant paw.

'Town house in Thorpe, isn't it,' Julee said.

'What's with that Shane?' somebody wondered.

It went without saying that nobody liked Shane. Back at school, or at the engineering shop, Gary seemed to remember that there had always been one person prepared to stand up for the weaselly kid, but somehow Shane had escaped this benediction. Other people had their defenders, but Shane now, he was merely universally loathed.

'You tell me,' Shirleen said. 'Got kicked out of Norwich School for a start.'

'Norwich School?'

'Fucking posh place down by the Cathedral.'

'What'd he get kicked out of there for?'

But what Shane had been expelled from Norwich School

for had to wait, for the man himself could now be glimpsed skulking through the side door that led into the bar, track-suited as ever, but with some fanciful new hair cut shaped like the top of a flat-iron. Of the many odd things about Shane, one of the oddest was that he had no self-consciousness. When he drew up level with them, he threw a shape and spun 180 degrees on the heels of his wedged trainers. 'Ladies. Rod . . .' His eye fell on Kenny. 'All right, Costessey boy?'

'Why don't you fuck off?' Julee demanded, and then, keeping it geographical: 'You Thorpe twat.'

Rodney went off to inspect the till. The girls got to their feet. Seeing that the feeling of the meeting was against him, Shane melted away.

❧

Every other Thursday after school finished, Gary took little Kayleigh round to her nan's for an hour. Mrs Thompson, Gary's mum - 75 now and looking it - lived on North Park Avenue. The routine was always the same: the insufficiently diluted Ribena out of pink-and-white-striped plastic tank-ards; the wire-haired terrier frantic behind the kitchen door; the heating set to stun. So, Gary had to allow, was the conversation.

'How's Lady Muck, if I might ask?'

'Don't start that again, Mum.'

'Not as if she comes round to see me, is it?'

'Not as if you come round and see her, is it either?'

Little Kayleigh, *My Little Pony* DVD unwatched, had already fallen asleep on the sofa. Outside the rain fell against the treble-glazed windows and a flight of rooks took off over

Eaton Park. Gary was bored with this interchange, just as he was pre-emptively bored with the one that usually followed it.

'And how are you making your living these days?' She was OK for her age, was Gary's mum, but she forgot things.

'I work in security, Mum. *You* know.'

'On the doors with that Kenny Sullivan?' She flung him a panoptic glance that took in the sleeping child, the juddering kitchen door and the photo of Gary's dad, besuited and melancholic, that lay on the mantelpiece next to the defunct clock and seemed to find fault with them all. 'Where's *he* living these days?'

'Bullus Road.'

'What's he want to live there for?' Mrs Thompson clasped her huge, rheumatism-wrecked hands before her in a vast, bony knot.

You could never win with his mum, Gary thought. Just as she had never liked Michaela for (allegedy) being too posh – something about the slice of lemon in the drink the first time she'd been round – so she had never liked Kenny for not being posh enough. In fact, as he now recalled, she'd had it in for Kenny from the moment they'd first lined up with the other cub scouts at Church Parade – you'd had to do things like that forty years ago, and you'd had to look as if you were enjoying them – and noticed that he was wearing gym shoes rather than a pair of regulation Startrite sandals.

'Is he still with that – what's her name – Celeste?'

'Jesus, Mum. They've been married for twenty years.'

Still, though, beneath Mrs Thompson's wrinkled exterior there lurked the vestiges of a human heart. When, 15 minutes later – the rain was still smearing the windows and the dog was still going ballistic in the kitchen – they were saying their farewells at the door and little Kayleigh had been gar-landed with her customary parting gifts (the mini-Mars Bars, the packet of Hula Hoops, the 50p piece – Gary's mum had not really kept up with inflation), some of the flame went out of her milky old eyes and, bending down to anoint little Kayleigh's curls with her moist old palm, she said: 'Next time you see that Kenny Sullivan, tell him I was asking about his little girl.'

'Why does nanna always have the heating on so *hot?*' little Kayleigh asked when they were back and she had (disdainful-ly) stowed the 50p piece away in the pocket of her windcheat-er. And Gary had wanted to say: because it was something your parents did, like not liking certain foods, and certain countries, and certain ethnic groups, and not realising that life changed while you didn't, and not liking, or sometimes very much disliking, certain of your friends, and not realis-ing that you went on hanging about with them *because they were your friends*, which was odd, really, when you thought about it, because presumably in that primordial never-never land when dinosaurs lurched across Eaton Park and there were pterodactyls taking flight over the UEA they had had friends themselves like that, who their parents had dispar-aged and who they'd stuck by out of loyalty, or cussedness or some other reason that they couldn't quite put into words. Instead he had stayed silent and driven them home through the avenues of crazed, wet tree and ricocheting car lights and the capering roadside shadows of a late October evening here beneath the ripening Norfolk sky.

That night he got to the Chariot to discover that Kenny had gone AWOL, that his place at the door had been filled by some goofball sent by the agency and that Shirleen reckoned it was because Carole had been taken to the Norfolk & Norwich that afternoon with a bad chest infection. All of which affected Gary so adversely that he found himself breaking the first un-written law of doormanship, giving some lippy kid in the line a tap and then, equally inexplicably and counter-intuitively, picking him up from the concrete, dusting him down and saying he hoped there were no hard feelings, which, merci-fully, the kid being startled by this unusual turn of events into a state of mute acquiescence, there weren't.

⁂

In any case, what had Gary's mum got to complain of? Reviewing an adolescence and early manhood spent in Kenny's company, Gary couldn't see what the fuss had been about. You did what you did and took the opportunities offered you. That was all. Early morning saunters, with lofted rucksacks, fags in hand, across the dewy grass of Eaton Park on the way to school. Going fishing with Mr Sullivan, Kenny's dad, in the trout lakes at Necton. Heading into town on Saturday morn-ings to check out the record shops and the vintage clothes store on the back of the market. Had Kenny ever said anything much? Gary couldn't remember. Had he ever said anything much in return? Gary didn't think so. Half the time you got by on inference and implication. You knew, instinctively, what the other person was thinking, or about to do, and you kept quiet, which meant, if anything, that the compact between you got deeper. 'Thick as thieves,' Kenny's dad had once said, watching the pair of them lug the fishing creel out of the boot of his car - Gary had always liked Mr Sullivan, who had none of his own parents' suspicion or guile - a statement which, while it acknowledged the ties that bound them, was also ominous in its way. For thieves, as Gary well understood, having known a few in his time, whatever their best efforts and the indifference of a case-hardened world, had a distressing tendency to get found out.

※

And then came that final Saturday evening on which, mysteriously, all these elements seemed to coalesce into a single point of focus, rather as if, Gary thought, you were watching a football match in which some directionless mid-field foul-up, with players flying in from all sides and the ball vanished beneath a scrum of vigorously contending bodies and the ref trying to make sense of half a dozen visible infringements, had suddenly broken apart and all that was left was the number nine, resourceful and unpoliced, defenders labouring vainly in his wake, bearing down on goal.

For a start Norwich had lost, which meant the atmosphere on the door had an edge and there were blokes in yellow and green shirts hurtling around looking for an excuse to kick something or someone. And then the chippy kids who were never going to make it through the Chariot's foyer in the first place seemed less susceptible to suasion ('No, mate, you're not coming in here, mate. Why not? Cos you're not properly dressed, mate. Don't get stroppy with me, mate. I'm just doing my job. All right, then, fuck off.') But really the problem was Big Kenny, who was checking his phone three times a minute, looking simultaneously tragic and half-submerged, as if he'd just materialised from out of the waves on Yarmouth beach with the seagulls crying above his head and the grey sky threatening to swallow him up. Another thing – possibly the worst thing – about Kenny at these times was that you couldn't talk to him. Gary had tried in the past and got nowhere. The big man just clammed up and stared you down and whatever you wanted to say took flight into the air above your head and whirled away with the breeze.

About ten it quietened down. The stroppy kids, the ones who'd try to square up to you chin to chin, even though they were six inches shorter and three stone lighter, had gone off to the Queen of Iceni or the bowling rink. There were still packs of girls coming in from the train station, barefoot, with their high-heeled shoes in carrier bags, but they weren't any trouble; in fact, you sometimes wanted to tell them that they were too young for a place like this and would be better off staying at home with their mums watching *Casualty* than throwing up in the Chariot's Domestos-scented toilet while their mates giggled outside the door. It was cold out here now and Gary slapped his gloved hands together, stared at the familiar horizon – the City Hall clock, bathed in mellow, refracted light, the spire of the cathedral – and felt the wind coming off the river against his newly-shaven cheek. Kenny, still silent, looked up from his texting, his latest glimpse into the unimaginable world of double-strength antibiotics, saline drips and drained lungs, that stretched out around him. Gary caught his eye and, emboldened, with the memory of Michaela and all those small-hours-stake-outs before him, said the only thing he could think of in the circumstances, which was: 'Praying for you, mate.'

Even then it would have been all right, sort of, out there in the dark with the wind coming in off the river, and the babble of voices rising from pavements further away, and the click of metal on stone as the girls stooped to put on their heels, and Rita ferrying them cups of tea (Gary said 'thanks, Reet'; Kenny said nothing.) Even then it would have been OK, had not the scrawny kid in the tracksuit and the beanie hat, with the Coke can dangling from his bony fingers, emerged out of the shadows and swayed towards them, a kid so nondescript that Gary had his palm extended and was on the point of saying 'No way, mate, you're not coming in here dressed like that,' when he realised that the apparition was, in fact, weaselly Shane. Even then it would have been all right, just about, had not Shane, as the pair of them stepped aside to let him through, yelled 'Costessey boys!' and then the two or possibly three words 'NR5!' Now, 'Costessey boys' you could let go. You could let that go. But 'NR5', the postcode that encompassed Costessey, Bowthorpe and one or two other choice suburban hamlets, Gary knew to be unforgiveable. It was Norwich shorthand. It meant food parcels and NSPCC inspectors. It meant bailiffs at the door and kids fencing with pool cues outside the Fiveways pub. It meant trouble. Trouble, especially, for whoever had said it.

It was a long time since Gary had seen the big man properly in action. Kenny gave a kind of seismic twitch, dropped his shoulder and then, almost lazily, swung out a fat hand that sent Shane sprawling onto the concrete, legs folded beneath him and making little whimpering sounds as he went. There would have been more – there would have been a lot more – but by now Gary was on the case, brisk and pacific, slapping down the second raised fist, getting his body in the way, in so far as you could get your body in the way of Big Kenny when he was off on one, and going 'No, mate,' and 'Steady on, mate,' and 'He's had enough, mate,' and even 'He's not worth it, mate,' and the other things you said on such occasions. And then things, which had been happening very quickly, suddenly slowed down. Shane, still whimpering and retching, crawled off into the club. Kenny gave Gary a bleak, hopeless glance and wandered away into the night. That left Gary alone at the door, looking at the splashes of blood Shane had left behind him and thinking that they'd both get sacked for this.

Long ages seemed to go by. He was so taken aback by what had passed that he let in a couple of burglars' dogs that he knew had just come to sell pills without so much as a blink. And then Mr Brannigan came outside and they stared at each other in the way you did when things like this happened. Mr Brannigan looked even wearier than usual. 'Not blaming you,' he said. 'Kid's a fucking disgrace. Where's that Kenny?'

'Gone off somewhere,' Gary said.

'Yeah, well,' Mr Brannigan said, almost hopelessly. Then, abruptly, his mood changed. 'Look,' he said. 'Fucker knocked out one of Shane's front teeth. Do me a favour and see if you can find it.'

Gary looked at the dozens of square feet of undifferentiated concrete. 'Could be anywhere,' he suggested.

'Just have a look, will you?' Mr Brannigan said, wearily. And so he got down on one knee, micro torch in hand – he always carried a torch on duty; you never knew who or what might go where – and played the beam over the grey stretch of the Chariot's frontage. There was more wind coming off the river – out there in the fields beyond Thorpe and Plumstead it would be blowing up a storm – and he could hear the traffic rumbling near the station. One by one, like smash-cuts in a film, the pictures stole into his head, pictures that came from here, there and everywhere: Carole's white face propped up against the dentist's chair; him and Kenny in their school gear tearing across the park; little Kayleigh staring as he picked up the spade; all of them rapt and expectant, poised and yet fearful, halfway between this world and whatever lay beyond it.

SOMEWHERE OUT THERE
WEST OF THETFORD

M RS GROTE LIVED on the last pitch of the final row of the park, squeezed up on four brick casters next to the barbed-wire fence and beneath the overhang of the elm trees. Some of the caravans had neat gravel surrounds and wind chimes that rattled constantly in the Breckland gales, but hers was just a big oblong box with the paint ribboning off the window frames and patches of withered grass where she threw out the tea leaves of a morning. The front half had no curtains and late at night you could see her long, angular torso bobbing around the living space or sitting bolt upright in a deckchair watching TV. The Grotes were Fen people who had headed east fifty years ago, and traces of this heritage lay around the caravan where there were, in addition to an eel hive, three or four rush baskets that could be folded up into themselves like a Panama hat. You could see it, too, in Mrs Grote's long-sightedness, the way in which she always seemed to be regarding something that was a hundred yards away, out on the edge of a bare horizon bounded by endless grey sky. She was a tall, gnarled woman in her late seventies with a brown-stained skin who looked as if she had been carved out of a tree, and conspicuous, even for the backwater in which she had come to rest.

Billy used to see her late in the afternoons, walking back along the verge from Brandon with her grocery bag, tottering a bit yet determined, not caring about the HGVs that went hurtling by on their way to Lynn. Sometimes there were two bags, which gave her equilibrium, and she swung them vigorously in either hand, like a porter carrying cases up a hotel stair-flight. On the third or fourth of these occasions, when the rain was coming down hard and the twilight was stealing up out of the road-side thickets, he stopped the van, leaned out of the nearside window and said: would she like a lift?

'I'll not say no,' she said, so he swept a hand down to displace the drift of newspapers and sweet wrappers from the passenger seat and reached over for the grocery bags, which mostly harboured packets of rice and tins of steak and kidney; the kind of things people who lived on caravan parks ate, he thought, and pretty much the contents of his own larder. The look on her face as she climbed in beside him told him that the lift was hers by right, that he had no other purpose in life except to drive her home.

'Seen you around the site, haven't I?' he said, in case she should think him to be some anonymous way-layer of old ladies.

'You might have,' she told him, and he was reminded of the women who had taught him at school, calm and indifferent, treating insult and olive branch alike with the same grave unconcern. For the rest of the journey – it was only a couple of miles down back lanes that were already melting into darkness – she sat rigid in her seat, saying nothing. Back at the park he took care to drive her right up to the door, which was on the row down from his own pitch, but the solicitousness went unmarked. 'I'll thank you again,' she said, bags balancing her big frame, not looking at him as she stepped out into the mud, and he watched her head away up the half-dozen wooden steps, prod at an envelope that the postman had left hanging in the slot that made do as a letter box and stand looking at it as if he and the van and everything else in the world had ceased to exist. Then, just as he was starting to back the van away down the path, she turned back on her heel to stare, the letter still in her hand, and he saw that he had done the right thing.

After that he started looking out for her, in a small way. He was elsewhere most of the time driving the oil truck out to Oxburgh, Wisbech, Soham, places even further afield, but sometimes, coming back of an evening, he'd leave a milk carton or a packet of Jaffa Cakes on the topmost step of the caravan, out of the wind, and be rewarded, next time he saw her, with another frosty nod. Mariette, who came over a couple of nights a week from Brandon, and to whom exchange was a two-way thing, was amused. 'What d'you want to give that old girl pints of milk for?' she wondered. 'Anyone can go get a pint of milk.' But Billy judged that he was responding to solitude, not need.

'She's got no one,' he rationalised. 'Or' – correcting himself – 'no one I know of.' That much was true. It was a wet autumn that year, darker too, and Mrs Grote, plodding home along the verges, bags in hand, looked more wraith-like than ever, gaunt and sepia-toned, as if she had just risen up from one of the beet fields that ran alongside the road. One afternoon, when he'd left a packet of digestives on the step, she asked him in for a cup of tea.

'Your name's Billy ent it?'

'Billy Martin.' The tea was a queer tan colour, but not the worst he'd had.

'You like eels?'

'Never have tasted them,' he conceded.

'You come round here one night,' she instructed, as if this was the greatest favour ever done by woman to man, 'and I'll cook you some eels. Can bring that girl, too, if you've a mind.'

But Mariette refused to go with him. She had better things to do than dine out in Mrs Grote's caravan. 'You're soft,' she said. 'You'll be painting up her windows next and not taking a penny.' Billy didn't like to admit that this idea had already occurred to him. The eels, like much else in this part of Norfolk, tasted of river water and woodsmoke, but he did his best. Mrs Grote fidgeted around the caravan, opening doors and closing them, putting kettles on to boil and then thinking twice. There were framed photographs on the damp wall of old men pulling sedge out of the Fen dykes, ancient families – the girls in pinafore dresses, the boys in flat caps and hob-nails – brought together before cottage doors. On the couch by the window the *Radio Times* lay open at the day's date with inked crosses running down the margin.

'You see after me,' she said, pronouncing it *arter* and accepting one of his hand-rolled cigarettes, 'and you won't lose.'

'Don't mind if I lose or not,' he said, a bit affronted by this directness.

Come November there were fewer people on the site and the days started earlier. Most mornings he was up and gone by 7, van parked up at the depot, taking the truck out on the A11, the A47 and the roads beyond it, up into Lincolnshire, westward into the square fields of blackened Fenland earth. The people he delivered to lived in odd places, on run-down farmsteads where no farming seemed to be done, down out-of-the-way lanes hedged with cow parsley where fallen branches crackled under the tyres. Mariette, thinking the oil-delivering foolish and underpaid, wanted him to get a job in town. Meanwhile, he was discovering things about Mrs Grote. One of them was that the floor of her caravan was slowly disintegrating into the mould of old leaves and litter beneath it. This could be fixed with some hammered-down squares of plywood, but there was nothing he could do about the second thing, which was Mrs Grote's habit of taking a turn.

The first time this occurred they were coming down the caravan steps together, so he could stop her fall and put her back on her feet. 'This happen before?' he asked, worried by the way her legs seemed to unravel beneath her.

'Now and again,' Mrs Grote allowed. But the second time was so bad that Billy was unable properly to rouse her from her chair and, in collaboration with Mr Morgan, the site's owner, brought the paramedics out from Thetford.

'You got anyone we ought to call?' Billy wondered, after the paramedics had been and gone, leaving instructions for Mrs Grote to attend her GP's surgery the following day.

'Could ring my *darter*,' Mrs Grote suggested, pulling a slip of paper out of the mass of old envelopes that lay next to her sink and indicating by the way in which she flopped down again in her chair that the job was Billy's.

Mrs Grote's daughter came over the next afternoon. She was a tall, surly woman with oiled-up hair raked back over her scalp who drove a battered estate car with a Stars and Bars transfer on the back window and a bumper sticker that said BEWARE: RATTLESNAKE INSIDE. Billy left them to it. When the woman came out a few minutes later, she gave him one of those disbelieving, are-you-still-here looks.

'I suppose you're one of the ones she said wouldn't lose.'

He jerked his shoulders, wanting to give as good as he got. 'No concern of mine what you think.'

'Well, she's not got anything to give, that's for sure,' the woman said, bitterly. He realised now that he had seen her before, and that she worked in one of the pubs in Brandon. But no glint of recognition dawned on the other side of the hedge.

'Don't you and her get on?' You got this a lot out here: women who never set eyes on sisters who lived in the next street; teenage boys camped out in hostels while their parents looked on. Everyone in west Norfolk seemed to be estranged from somebody.

'Do me a favour,' she said as she got back into the estate car, whose rear end, he now saw, was half-fallen away and held together with streaks of solder. 'Don't phone me unless it's real bad, OK?'

He decided that he would get back at Mrs Stars and Bars somehow, that he owed it to Mrs Grote and the eel hives and the pictures of the old men out ditching and dredging, this dead world in which she now played no part. December came and things slowed down. The beet fields were picked clean, and the rooks sat in the leafless trees not bothering to explode into flight if they heard a noise. Out across the meadows the weakening sun caught the mist and pulsed through it, turning the landscape ghost-like and ominous. Mariette was supposed to be coming for Christmas, but her texts had dried up. The people he delivered to had started to give him presents now: jars of jam; bottles of home-made wine; plastic boxes of chicken wings from Tesco. He left the non-perishable gifts in a heap on his fold-up table like pirates' plunder

'What's the matter with your daughter?' he asked once

– they were out at Castle Acre, to which she had consented to be driven one Sunday afternoon. The fog was coming in from the west. Up there on the escarpment, dozens of feet above the crumbling stone, they looked like a pair of medieval sentries staring out across the debatable lands where warring armies lurked.

'Never had anything to say to each other,' she said. He knew he was lucky to get this far. His own mother would not have said as much. He thought for a moment she was going to have one of her turns, sink down onto the wet grass and start gasping for breath, but unexpectedly she righted herself and they went back to the van.

The park had not forgotten Christmas. There were fairy lights up in two or three of the caravans that remained occupied, and Mr Morgan had erected a Christmas tree inside the front gate with a plastic star stapled to its topmost branch. He got the text from Mariette on Christmas Eve as he stood inspecting the oven-ready turkey in its plastic sack, worrying what you did with it. No details were offered beyond the apology, but Billy knew what had happened. Like the storms, which cruised up from the Wash in angry clouds that were visible thirty miles away, he had seen it coming. Hastening over to Mrs Grote's caravan – she might not care to join him over the turkey, but she would like to be asked – he found her tossed to one side of the deckchair with her eyes off at a slant, so that was that. He called the ambulance and told Mr Morgan in his shack and then went away, thinking that whatever happened next was none of his business.

Later, when the dusk was welling up in the field-bottoms and the breeze had begun to agitate the wind chimes, he went back to the caravan and, finding that no one had bothered to fasten the door, stole guiltily inside. One or two things that he had missed that morning – a solitary paper chain hung over the far wall, a row of Christmas cards on the shelf next to the cooker – now caught his eye. Wanting to feed his curiosity about Mrs Grote, the person she was and the things she owned, he bent down and opened the big cupboard on the cooker's further side. Here there were a dozen empty whisky bottles and about the same number of steak and kidney pie tins. He was wondering about taking one of the pies on the grounds that it would be preferable to the turkey when he saw the scuffed-up padded bag. On the front, in big, flagrant capitals, Mrs Grote, or someone else, had written JEANNIE GROTE, and he realised that in all the time this had been going on he had never known her name.

'OK, Jeannie Grote,' he said quietly to the silent caravan, feeling the notes crinkle in his hands. There were not so many of them, but they were high-denomination – twenties and fifties; about £1200 in all, he reckoned. He rolled them into a wedge that filled the space in the palm of his hand, took a sip from the half-inch of liquor that remained in one of the whisky bottles and then put them back in the bag. Later still, when the evening was far advanced and even the light in Mr Morgan's cubbyhole had been extinguished, he crept out of the front gate, where the Christmas tree had lurched slightly to one side and was shedding its needles, went fifty yards down the road and cast the padded bag into a storm drain, gripped by an emotion that was not quite grief and not quite exhilaration, but something else, something sharp and combustible, flaring up into the dense Norfolk sky.

THE BOY AT THE DOOR

IT WAS THE summer of 1974 and I would have been
13 going on 14, sitting in the cramped back room of my
parents' house with the lunch things just cleared away, wondering how to pass the long, hot August afternoon that lay
ahead when, twenty feet away at the front of the house, the
doorbell rang. And my mother, hastening from the kitchen
to answer it, spent what seemed to be an unusually long time
talking in a low, indistinguishable voice to whoever had arrived
there and then came into the back room with a rather peculiar
expression on her face and said: 'There's a boy at the door.'

'What sort of a boy?'

'I don't recognise him,' my mother said, a bit hopelessly,
'but he wants to speak to you.'

I could see instantly – we both could – the strangeness of
the situation, as we stood there in the airless room with the
white surface of the Bakelite radio gleaming in the sunshine
and the picture of my father in his masonic apron looking
even more sinister than usual. The boys I knew did not,
by and large, turn up unannounced on the doorstep. They
telephoned in advance and made arrangements. Even when
they did blow in from nowhere, parking their bikes on the
front lawn or propping them up against the garage door, my
mother knew who they were, could greet them familiarly, ask
after their parents and for the bikes to be removed from the
front lawn, and slot them into the world she knew. This was
unprecedented.

As I stepped out into the hall, the faint hint of a breeze came in through the open door to stir the pile of newspapers and neatly slit-open envelopes that always lay on a chair beneath the telephone. The boy still stood on the doorstep, not front-ways on and filling the space as most people would have done, but slightly to one side with one shoulder hunched against the brickwork. He had a soft, bulbous nose, rather frog-like features and looked as if at some point in his life someone had ordered him about a lot. Such was the oddity of this visitation that it took me several seconds to identify him as a boy called Terry Runacles, who had briefly, a couple of years ago, turned up at the Scout troop where I was a member, spent two or three weeks at its meetings, and then left it in circumstances that had not been explained. Had I ever spoken to him? Yes, I had. We had both been on the trip to the local chocolate factory and he had sat next to me on the bus. So, reaching the door, I stared at him in a way that was neither friendly nor reproving but simply non-committal, waiting to see what he would say and what he wanted. And Terry, jerking his shoulder away from the stanchions of the door, so that the black sweater he wore, which was both too big for him and too hot for the day, snagged on the brick, loomed into view and said: 'I was just going by, so I thought I'd come and see you.'

He was very red in the face and had the makings of a bum-fluff moustache under his bulbous nose. 'Good to see you Terry,' I said, for I was a polite boy, conscious of what I owed to the people around me, not least my mother, who was still waiting, a bit distractedly, by the telephone shelf. And then, because it seemed the most reasonable thing to do in the circumstances, while also gesturing at the annoyance I felt at being disturbed in the school holidays by such a boy as Terry Runacles, I added, 'I didn't know you knew where I lived.'

But Terry had this one covered. 'Matty Collier told me,' he explained, referring to another boy from the Scout troop. 'He's at my school.'

He was still looming in front of me, big and shambling, like the Honey Monster in the Sugar Puffs ad, and I was about to tell him that I was busy, or about to go out, when my mother, in that indescribably arch way in which parents sometimes give instructions to their children in the presence of third parties, said: 'Aren't you going to invite your friend in?'

I could see her point. Terry was not by any stretch of the imagination my friend – we both knew that – but the dictates of bourgeois civility meant that he couldn't be left indefinitely on the doorstep snagging his baggy black sweater on the brick while life went on around him. All the same, I knew that I did not want him in the house, that the thought of Terry Runacles, with his bum-fluff moustache and his frog face at large in my bedroom inspecting the shelf of dusty Airfix kits and the back numbers of *Look and Learn*, was insupportable to me. And so, decisively, grabbing Terry by the arm, nodding at my mother and stepping out onto the doorstep I said, 'Let's go for a walk.'

And there we were, suddenly, out on the garden path, where it was hotter than ever and the laurel hedge, untrimmed for the past three years, cast immense oblongs of shadow onto the gravel. Silently we covered the ten yards or so to the gate and came out onto The Avenues, the long arterial road that led all the way from the city's edge to the university and the semi-rural Norwich suburbs. And here I saw that Terry, mysteriously, was at a loss. On the doorstep, with an aim in view, he had acted with a certain amount of self-possession. Now, having captured me and brought me away, he had no idea what to do with me. He was, I now saw, sweating profusely – far more than was warranted by the heat of the afternoon; there were huge blobs of perspiration on his tallowy forehead. And so, in unspoken agreement, we turned left and headed up The Avenues, where the middle-class housing soon gave out and the council estates loomed into view. A car went by – not a particularly glamorous car, belching fumes out of its exhaust pipe – and Terry said, almost fiercely, clipping his vowels in his eagerness to get the words out, 'D'you like cars?'

'Not very,' I said. My father drove thrifty Citroen Ami-8s of such negligible horse-power that on steep hills the rest of the family would have to get out and traipse behind. 'Do you?'

'If I had a car I'd drive to Peterborough and see my sister,' Terry said.

'Does your sister live in Peterborough?'

'I think so,' Terry said and then fell silent, and I saw that I had been wrong to press him about his sister who may have lived in Peterborough and should have kept my curiosity – which was not really curiosity, but only politeness - to myself.

By this point we had reached the shops at Bunnett Square, still silent in the afternoon sun, for the crowds only began to gather when the first edition of the *Eastern Evening News* arrived at the newsagent's shop. Here, I assumed, Terry would cease his forced march. He would be the kind of boy seduced by the lure of shop windows. He would want to hang around the sweetshop or loiter in the doorway of Davies's, the grocery on the far side, observing the people who came in and out. Instead he crossed over the road and headed north past the Earlham Branch Library, where there were women with prams and small children gathered by the gate and a jangling ice-cream van pulled up on the verge. The sight of the ice-cream van stirred Terry to speech. 'Have a sweet,' he said, affably, pulling a roll of something out of his trouser pocket. They were very old fruit pastilles that had crystallised into little nodules of sugar, but I prised one out and chewed on it while the traffic thundered down Colman Road and Terry stood on the grass outside the library with a kind of haunted, storm-wracked look, as if several possibilities, none of them very agreeable, were clamouring for his attention and he could not choose between them. For my own part, I wondered how many more minutes would have to go by before I could decently leave him, congratulate myself that I had conciliated whatever whim had driven him to our front door and set off gladly for home. But suddenly something seemed to strike him and he rocked on his heels – he was wearing a pair of big, well-worn wedge shoes – and said, out of nowhere, 'D'you like school?'

This, naturally, was impossible to answer, or rather impossible to answer honestly. In fact, I did like school. I liked it very much, and I was looking forward to four more years at it before I went off to university. But I knew that this was not something I could say to Terry Runacles and would have trouble admitting even to the boys I was at school with. 'It's all right,' I said.

'I hate school,' Terry said, with a kind of elephantine savagery. 'My dad says I can leave when I'm sixteen and join the Merchant Navy.'

'Oh yes?' I had no idea what anybody did in the Merchant Navy. 'Where will you go?'

But this was too much for Terry. 'I don't know,' he said. 'Canada and places like that, I expect.'

The women with their prams and children had moved off. The surface of the patch of asphalt on which we lingered was melting in the heat. Terry brought the toe of one of his worn wedge shoes down hard and looked at the impression it made. By this stage I had had enough of him. I bore him no ill-will, but I had had enough of him. There was still a tiny, unswallowable fragment of the crystallised fruit pastille in my mouth and I spat it out. Solemnly, Terry watched the spittle fall. 'We could go round to mine,' he said, unexpectedly.

'Where's that?' Terry could live anywhere – Hethersett, Bowthorpe, South Park Avenue. It was as well to know what you were letting yourself in for.

'Stannard Road,' he said, pointing to one of the side streets on the other side of the main thoroughfare. If he had lived half or even a quarter of a mile away I would have said no, but an invitation to a house a hundred yards distant was ungainsayable. We waited for a gap in the traffic and sprinted over Colman Road.

And now, I saw, with a certain amount of unease, our relationship had changed. Back on home ground, stealing past the cars parked up on Stannard Road's scuffed verge, he was surer of himself. A small boy popped up from behind a gate like a jack-in-the-box and Terry nodded at him curtly like a mafioso recognising an underling on the Chicago broadwalks. Here in Stannard Road he regarded me as an accomplice, ready to join him in whatever schemes he had planned, loyal to the last. Terry's house lay at the far end, the fifth of six identical semi-detacheds drawn up in an elliptical line. The smell of sulphur from the May & Baker factory hung over the tiny garden. Terry reached under a flower pot that lay to the left of the front step and opened the door. There was no one about. Safe inside his own domicile, he looked suddenly nonplussed, a bit uncertain, as if several of the place's essential elements had been altered in his absence. Then he recovered himself and ploughed on into the living room, where there were a couple of armchairs and a horsehair sofa with the stuffing bursting out in half a dozen places. He was breathing heavily again, but seemed quietly satisfied, pleased to have got me into the house, proud of the amenities it offered. At the same time there was something odd about the room we had fetched up in, so odd that it took me a moment or two to establish why its atmosphere was so peculiar. It was not that there was hardly anything in it – apart from the sofa and the chairs the furnishings consisted of a portable TV on a stand, an occasional table and some pieces of *bric-á-brac* – more that what there was had been so meticulously arranged. Thus, the chairs were at precise forty-five degree angles to the sofa, six feet apart, and the line of glass elephants on the mantelpiece were planted at exact, six-inch intervals. The walls were bare apart from a framed photograph of Terry and a man and woman in middle age – presumably his parents – which had been over-lit, so that their faces reared up out of it, stark and horrified, as if some terrible tragedy were taking place a few feet in front of them.

All this was faintly disconcerting and, it seemed to me, deliberate. Design had created this scene, not poverty. I might have been a middle-class boy from a comfortable house, but I knew poverty when I saw it and I knew that this was something else altogether. And now, seated in this curious, regimented room - Terry on the horsehair sofa, myself on one of the chairs - I wondered exactly what we were supposed to do. For there were no Monopoly boxes under the TV, no sideboards crammed with blow-football kits or jigsaw puzzles, no record players and racks full of vinyl singles - nothing. But the thought that, having succeeded in luring a guest to his home, he now had a duty to entertain him seemed not to have occurred to Terry. Leaning back against the horsehair sofa with his pudgy hands clasped behind his back and the sweat still standing out on his big slab of a forehead, he seemed perfectly happy, as if, against long odds, he had achieved a feat so unexpected and considerable that the immediate future could look after itself. Presently he got up, went out to the kitchen, crashed around opening doors and closing them for a while and came back with half a packet of rather stale custard cream biscuits. We ate them one by one, staring at the glass elephants in their unwavering line.

All this time, I now suspect, I was trying to fit Terry, the house in Stannard Road, the minimalist surrounding and even the musty packet of biscuits, into a wider context of other afternoons spent with other boys in other houses. Admittedly, some of these had not been without their incidental oddities. There had been boys who had obscure hobbies, like stone-polishing or collecting bus tickets. There were boys whose idea of a good time was to spend four hours playing dice cricket. But set against this band of eccentrics and solipsists, Terry was in a class of his own. I had met no one like him, seen nothing like the interior of his house or the complete absence of paraphernalia with which, it seemed to me, life had to be supported. Enormous stretches of time seemed to pass in the room while we slowly ate the biscuits and I sat – a little mesmerised now by the heat and the inertia – staring at Terry and waiting for something to happen, some cue I could grasp at, something that would give this traipse along The Avenues to Stannard Road in the August sunshine a sense of purpose and fulfilment. Finally, after what seemed like hours, Terry shifted himself forward on the sofa, opened his mouth and closed it like a goldfish, opened it again and said with a dreadful gravity: 'My mum's just died. My dad's out making the arrangements. That's why there's no one here.'

'What did she die of?'

Terry pondered this for a moment. 'Pneumonia,' he said. There was a faint suggestion in this that he thought I might not believe him, but it seemed fair enough to me. People died of pneumonia, just as they died of lung cancer and peritonitis.

'I'm sorry,' I said, 'about your mother.'

'We don't know when the funeral is,' Terry said. 'I expect it'll be next week. Anyway, I shan't have to go to school.'

It seemed far hotter in Terry's front room than anywhere I had ever been in my life. Having got the information about his mother dying out, Terry seemed to relax. His eyes flickered a little and he slapped the front of his sweater once or twice as if there were small creatures in there beneath the folds that needed subduing.

'Did your mother want you to join the Merchant Navy?'

'Yes, she did,' Terry said, a bit less confidently. 'She said I ought to see the world.' But the thought of seeing the world seemed to depress him. On the one or two occasions I had taken any notice of him at the Scout troop he had looked like this: crestfallen, suspicious, oppressed by unseen enemies.

'I didn't like the Scouts,' he said, as if suddenly divining what I was thinking about.

'Why not? Why didn't you like them?'

'I don't know. I just didn't.'

'What did you think it was going to be like?'

'I don't know,' Terry said, obstinately. 'I just didn't like them.' Then, unexpectedly, he cheered up again. 'Here,' he said. 'You can look at this if you like.'

As I looked on, he jerked up one of the cushions of the horsehair sofa, scrabbled around in some concealed space towards the back and brought out a pornographic magazine. Clearly the magazine had come in for some rough treatment in the past as its spine had been bound up with Sellotape. It was far dirtier than the ones that got handed round at school. Within its stained and lurid cover, weary-looking men with enormous penises made free of well-proportioned but curiously inert girls on kitchen tables and on the bonnets of cars. I inspected it for a while without much interest. When I looked up it was to find that Terry, still breathing heavily, had gone to sleep on the sofa. His frog face had composed itself into softer lines and, as he exhaled, the gusts of air set the strands of his bum-fluff moustache crawling back and forth. For a moment I wondered what to do about the magazine. If I left it on the unoccupied part of the sofa, there was a chance that Terry's father would come back and find it. On the other hand, Terry's father might well be its owner. In the end, not without difficulty, I prised up one of the cushions and slid it back inside.

All this required a fair amount of disturbance, but still Terry slept on. From outside the window I could hear the late-afternoon life of Stannard Road starting up. There were car doors slamming, the sound of loud voices suddenly falling away as their owners stepped through front doors and side-gates. Standing in the doorway of the Runacles' living room, I took a last look at Terry, whose mother had died, and who had disliked the Scouts, hated school and wanted to join the Merchant Navy, and had a copy of *Cunning Stunts* concealed in his sofa, for I knew that I would never speak to him again, or he to me, that whatever compact we had sealed between us that afternoon would never be renewed. Thinking about it afterwards, ten or even twenty years later, I realised that I had fundamentally misjudged him, that all the time I had wanted to see him as a symbol of something – exclusion, ostracism, class, who knew what? – when all he really represented was himself. And in fact, only a month later, at a safe distance in Bunnett Square, I saw him with a woman who to judge from the faint facial likeness and the exasperated gestures she directed at him could only have been his mother. And so I turned on my heel, shut the door carefully behind me and set off back down Colman Road and along the Avenues towards the familiar world that had been allotted me, that world of high teas and Startrite sandals and the *Morecambe and Wise Show*, settled destinies and – it had to be allowed – boredom.

FUN WITH DICK
AND JANE

THE PARGETERS WERE only a quarter of a mile away, so they walked it through the twilight. This was a desirable thing to do as it took them past several local landmarks that could not be properly inspected through a car window. The Pargeters' house was the most expensive in the village, but not for that reason the best appointed. The back garden was overhung by a gargantuan stretch of deodars that some previous owner had thought would do as a wind-break and a truck full of aggregate had once come to grief on the over-narrow drive.

'What did you say you thought of – Jeremy, is it?' Henrietta asked as they tramped purposefully along, putting out occasional hands to fend off the encroaching cow parsley.

'Rather minor public school,' Giles said, who had never been anywhere near any kind of public school but prided himself on his grasp of social detail.

'Whatever do you mean by that?'

Giles wondered what he did mean by it. Social codes were difficult to explain to anyone beyond the furnace in which they were forged. Choosing his words carefully, he said: 'Oh, you know, a bit assertive, a bit dogmatic. I mean, he told me you can get to Shropham along that backway and everyone knows you can't.'

'Well I've driven down there several times,' Henrietta said,

a fallen branch from a beech tree savaged in the last equinoc-
tial gale snapping under her feet, and he bowed his head, as he
always did, at his wife's rebuke. They had lived in this part of
Norfolk for a decade and a half, and he felt himself becoming
meeker and more self-effacing from one year to the next.

As they reached the lip of the Pargeters' gravel drive, a
tiny walkway that broke unexpectedly through the leylandii
hedge, a security light went on above their heads. 'That's
new,' Henrietta said, with the slightly suspicious tone she
brought to leaflets on the parish noticeboards offering lifts to
the elderly or help with their shopping. Rounding the bend in
the path, they found the front door open, a tiny dog rooting
around in the daffodil bed and a burly, red-faced man standing on the doorstep.

'My wife, Henrietta,' Giles said, a bit stiffly, as they came
up. Another light went on somewhere over to the right, dis-
closing that the garage doors had been repainted in bright,
arsenical green and that two gigantic porphyry pots had
taken the place of the old water butt. 'Darling, this is Richard
Pargeter.'

'Call me Dick,' the burly man said earnestly, as if this was
the greatest compliment anyone appearing at his front door
on an October evening had ever been paid.

There was a woman lurking just inside the door, her face
and figure indistinguishable in the complicated mixture of
light and shade produced by what looked like a halogen lamp
and some blackout curtains, who now edged cautiously out
onto the steps. 'Jane Pargeter,' she said, giving an odd little
twist to the final syllable, so that it came out as *Parget-ah*.'
She was small and slight to the point of being practically elfin,
and the contrast between her and the big, red-faced man was

so marked that it was as if they had done it deliberately and for comic purposes, like a Hollywood director casting Meryl Streep and Danny DeVito alongside each other in a romcom.

'Well, come in, come in,' Mr Pargeter said briskly, as if they were purposely holding things up and it was all he could do not to administer a rebuke. 'I'll just hoof the blasted dog out of the shrubbery and then we'll, we'll . . .'

He was one of those people, Giles realised, who never finished their sentences. This was not a good sign. Neither were the family portraits that hung on the wall of the vestibule to which they were now admitted: supple boys in smart jackets; big-bosomed girls with cow-like features sitting placidly at tea tables with their hands folded in their laps. The blasted dog had been hoofed out of the shrubbery by now and came scampering over their feet. 'This rascal is called Dido,' Mr Pargeter said, as if committees of dog-lovers had set in conclave to give the animal its name. 'Ate a bloody pincushion the other night. Had to take it to the emergency vets at Fakenham.'

'It was only a very small pincushion,' Jane glossed, 'but even so.'

They were in the sitting room now, where the riot of fresh sensations was almost too bewildering to be taken in. The Oldroyds, who had owned the house previously, had gone in for lime-green walls decorated with Hockney prints and views of old cathedrals, and long, low, quaintly-antimacassared sofas. The Pargeters, alternatively, had clearly spent a small fortune furnishing the room with antique club fenders and comfortless high-back armchairs that defied you to sit on them. There was a substantial bookcase where the Oldroyds had kept their sideboard full of china whose contents suggested that Mr Pargeter liked old-fashioned thrillers and studies of the Third Reich. But here they were, anyway, drinking glasses of the Pargeter's sparkling wine ('Have some fizz'), which Mr Pargeter presented with a little flourish, as if he had missed his vocation as a *sommelier*, talking about what people tended to talk about here, which was the amenities of village life.

'Actually,' Jane said, who Giles had previously assumed to be entirely under her husband's thumb but had since threatened to strike out on lines of her own, 'we nearly bought a house at Forncett St Peter. But it turned out that the surgery was three miles away.'

'Need a GP handy at my age,' said Mr Pargeter, who did not look more than sixty-five. 'What with all these . . . all these . . .' Not absolutely discouraged by his wife, he began to list the medical conditions from which he suffered and the treatments that had been prescribed. Giles occupied the time by examining an engraving of Putney Bridge executed in 1825 by someone with a defective sense of scale that hung on the wall a foot above his head. 'Not to mention these little chaps,' said Mr Pargeter, whipping out his two big fists and looking as if he meant to do some serious damage with them, and displaying a cluster of horny nodules at the base of each thumb.

'How are you finding the village?' Henrietta asked, with an artificial brightness that Giles knew meant trouble.

'We had lunch at the pub the other day,' Mr Pargeter said. 'Not really an experience I'd care to repeat.'

'I liked it,' Jane said mildly.

'They didn't cook the beef long enough,' Mr Pargeter went on mournfully. 'Seemed all right to begin with, and then . . . and then . . .' Giles, looking at the photos exhibited around the room, was struck by their adversarial juxtapositions. Just as you thought Mr Pargeter had gained the upper hand with an outsize portrait of himself in check trousers and tam o'shanter bent over a golf putter, so Mrs Pargeter popped up before a bunch of rose bushes at the Chelsea Flower Show to confound him. They were being ushered through into the dining room now – this, he noted, was pretty much as the Oldroyds had left it – watching Jane dawdle back and forth with a soup tureen. Mr Pargeter, seating himself at the head of the table, began to cram bread rolls into his mouth, a lump at a time.

The soup turned out to be reasonably good. While he was attending to it he heard Jane and Henrietta trading information about their respective daughters ('Such a nice young man, we thought . . . Works in library supply . . . Bound to settle down soon') and their husbands' previous careers (Mr Pargeter, he learned, had been and was still peripherally employed in re-insurance.) Having disposed of the bread, and eaten his bowl of soup so quickly that it seemed to vanish from his plate, Mr Pargeter reverted to the subject of village life.

'Of course, everywhere's like everywhere else these days. That's the pity of it. I mean, I was driving back the other day when I came across some twit riding one of those motorised scooters down the middle of the street.'

'I don't think he was a twit,' Jane said. 'It's quite legal to ride a motorised scooter.' The tone of her voice had changed from mild remonstrance to pretty serious chiding.

'A twit,' Mr Pargeter said. He was carving the duck now with surprising dexterity, as if he had been born to the task. 'Knows the things are dangerous but still scoots around the village scaring old ladies.'

'Not a twit,' Jane said, even more sharply.

'I mean,' Mr Pargeter said, changing the subject abruptly, 'what do you do in the evenings? We tried that man who was lecturing about medieval Norfolk at the parish hall, and he . . . and he . . .'

What did they do in the evenings, Giles wondered. But Mr Pargeter did not look like the kind of man who would warm to the topic of Jane Austen box sets and Scrabble marathons. 'Oh, we have our resources,' he said.

Henrietta had caught the scent of Jane's dissatisfaction. 'You see,' she said, with a little flicker of ulterior motive that Mr Pargeter really should have caught, 'we've always enjoyed spending time in each other's company.'

The duck was less nice than it looked, but they plugged gamely away. Giles thought of his study and his books about Anglo-Saxon field settlement and wild fowling in the Breckland. Why did anyone ever think that social life made a change from the domestic round?

'Do you like reading?' Jane asked very quietly. There was steam rising off the vegetables that Mr Pargeter had just heaped onto her plate and her face, with its emerald earrings and carefully sculpted eyebrows, looked suddenly ancient and witch-like, stricken in some odd and indefinable way. Outside the mist was rising up out of the hedges and the night was settling in. He was about to say that he did and that he liked nothing better when Mr Pargeter suddenly raised his hand from his plate and, like a dinosaur calling to its mate across a primeval swamp, said:

'The new Bill Bryson is jolly good. I bought it for Jane, but she only likes thrillers.'

Instinctively Giles knew that some line had been crossed, that nothing – not the pictures in their frames, the shine of the Pargeters' dinner service or the laws of hospitality – could prevent what was going to happen next. He could see, too, that Jane had experience in these matters and would know that timing was everything. She waited several seconds, long enough for Mr Pargeter to feel – if such thoughts ever occurred to him – that he had got away with this, might venture, now that the coast was clear, to some other subject, before slamming her glass of wine down on the table-top with such force that the top broke away from the stem and saying – no, practically shrieking – 'Why don't you shut up, you fat fuck?'

Thankfully, Henrietta had always known how to handle herself in these situations. 'Oh dear,' she said. 'Oh dear. Giles!' And Giles saw she was referring to the little pool of red wine that had leaked onto the edge of the white tablecloth. Obediently, he took the salt cellar and began to sprinkle the contents over the small, bloody puddle. Chastened but fascinated, Mr Pargeter watched him do it.

Later, torches to hand, the owls swooping out of the beech trees above their head, they walked back along the path. Giles wondered what the Pargeters were doing now that their guests had gone. Were they throwing plates at each other? Had they lapsed into sulky silence? Or had they settled their differences and decided to get on with the washing-up? It was hard to tell. Meanwhile, his own home with its Jane Austen box sets and its books about wild fowling in the Brecks, drew him back like a magnet.

'I think I could just about bring myself to send them a Christmas card,' Jane said. 'But I don't ever want them in my house . . . That poor man,' she added as an afterthought.

LADS FROM STRAT

'**O**F COURSE, THERE'S hardly such a thing as a genuine rural culture any more,' Mr Ferris said, drumming his fingers angrily on the table top, which magnified the sound in some obscure way and made it sound like someone doing 'noises off' of approaching horses with a couple of coconut shells. He was a tall, hunched man in his late fifties with a scatter of receding hair that had been dyed an odd chestnut colour. 'Certainly not round here. All gone with the Barrett homes and satellite TV and the flight from the land. There are no agricultural labourers now. Just people to drive the combines at harvest time.'

There were people who said that Mr Ferris was too highbrow to be station manager of Norfolk FM and that he would have been better off working for the BBC. But Simon rather liked him and enjoyed listening to his stories of how he had begun his career in TV drama bringing cups of tea to Dame Judi Dench. Thinking that Mr Ferris probably had a lot more to say about the decline of rural culture, he stared hard through the Perspex surround where, twenty feet away, the morning's broadcasting was getting into gear. Over in the corner studio he could see Rossy Boy, a.k.a. the Ross-meister, bouncing up and down in his chair as he cackled into the microphone. Nearer at hand, three stolid, put-upon girls seated before a line of telephones were taking calls from benighted villages out on the flat. Simon knew that the callers were always the same people: Harvey from Hempnall, Marjorie from Stratton Strawless, the lady from Corpusty who had to be shushed when she tried to talk about immigration. He shortened the focus of his gaze and examined other familiar artefacts: the wall-hung photographs of the Norfolk FM 'DJ Posse'; the piles of cardboard boxes; the crate of bottled water that had been lying there for a fortnight and was still waiting for someone to come and take it away.

'So what have you got for us this afternoon?' Mr Ferris wondered, without much enthusiasm. Simon knew, or thought that he knew, that this was a feint, for he and Mr Ferris were allies, united by the seriousness with which they went about things. There would be no phone-ins from pubs or reports from dwile-flonking competitions if they had their way. Over in the corner studio, Rossy Boy had stopped cackling into the microphone and, with huge enthusiasm, was playing a Buck's Fizz single from 1983.

'Well,' he began, cautiously, 'this afternoon's heritage village is Clenchwarton. We're going to get the lollipop lady from the local primary school. And then Professor Trunnion – you know, the linguistics expert - is coming in to do his dialect master-class. Oh, and the "What Happened in Norfolk" feature will be getting up to 1994.'

'What did happen in Norfolk in 1994?'

'I think the it was the year the Norwich Central Library burned down.'

'This I like,' Mr Ferris said, who always said this whether he liked it or not. 'How are you getting on with the local personalities?'

'I saw a couple of them yesterday. There's another one coming in tomorrow.'

The local personalities spot was a new idea of Mr Ferris's.

The people who applied to be on it had names like the Buttercup Boy and Sheringham Stevie. They wore picturesque clothing, spoke in exaggerated rustic accents and said things like: 'Whatever are you like?'

'Any of them any good?' Mr Ferris wondered hopefully.

'Not really.'

'Never mind. There's gold in them thar hills,' Mr Ferris said, reverting to his second signature remark.

Outside the window the pale East Anglian sky was streaking over with grey. Simon, who had been hoping that Mr Ferris was going to say that he was entering him for one of the local radio awards, wandered off along the long, serpentine passageway where Rossy Boy, his show now complete, stood awkwardly balanced against the granite-slab wall tying the lace of one of his sneakers. His real name was Ross Boythorn and he held the station record for the number of times you could smuggle the phrase 'Norfolk 'n' Good' onto the airwaves without the management noticing.

'Did you like the programme, Simon?' No Norfolk FM presenter ever passed another in a corridor without seeking reassurance on this point.

'I loved it.' Ross's twisty, anxious face went pink with gratitude. 'But where was the lady from Corpusty?'

'Oh, she was so furious this morning that Angie wouldn't let her past the switchboard.'

❦

The afternoon show passed without incident. The lollipop lady from Clenchwarton; Professor Trunnion; the man who did the historical look-backs: none of them cared to disappoint.

Afterwards Simon bought two small dressed Cromer lobsters from the stall on the market and took them back to the flat, where Myfanwy sat amidst her box files. When she saw him she made a little pawing motion in the dead air like the MGM lion.

'What sort of a day did you have?'

'Not bad.' Myfanwy was finishing her PhD at the local university. 'Fifteen hundred words. But then I had to edit out a lot of stuff about Sylvia Plath.' Her eye fell on the plastic bag. 'Why did you go and buy those? You know I can't eat sea food.'

She was a tall, thin girl who had her hair cut in the style of Virginia Woolf and sincerely hoped that at some point somebody would pay her money to teach graduate students how to write poetry. He took the lobsters, the salt cellar and the vinegar bottle into the sitting room and ate them both himself, while browsing through a book called *Norfolk Days and Norfolk Ways* that had caught his eye in a second-hand shop. He had always assumed that eventually he would find a girl like one of the ones in George Eliot's novels – sober and precise, of rare and discriminating taste – but somehow he had ended up with Myfanwy. Later, when Myfanwy had eaten some scrambled eggs, phoned her mother and sent half a dozen neurotic text messages to her supervisor, they sat by the gas fire watching a Japanese anime film in which a succession of sad-eyed ghosts wandered through trackless oriental skies. It was a blustery night and he thought of the wind buffeting in across the coastal villages - Sea Palling, Scratby and Winterton – telephone wires undulating in the breeze, the distant boom of the North Sea surf, the marram grass tremulously aflutter.

'Professor Habbakuk says there's a job coming up at Aberystwyth and I ought to apply for it,' Myfanwy said, a bit diffidently, as they were getting ready for bed, struggling to put her arms through the sleeves of her long white nightgown.

'I've got another one of those local personalities coming in tomorrow,' he said, determined to give as good as he got.

&

Sid the Ratcatcher – this was the name he had given at reception - was a small, self-contained man in what might have been his early seventies, with dark, weather-beaten skin, cross-hatched with deeply-engraved wrinkles, and a fan of white hair that stood up on the top of his head like a turkey-cock. Whereas other candidates – the Buttercup Boy and Sheringham Stevie – had come, as it were, in costume, dressed in voluminous smocks or tarry sailors' sweaters, Sid the Ratcatcher was less conspicuously attired in a check sports jacket and brown corduroy trousers. He was also more talkative.

'Don't mind my asking,' Simon said, 'but do you actually catch rats?'

The Ratcatcher grinned, as if to acknowledge that this was a fair question. 'I catched a few in my time. Now and again. But mostly it was rabbits. We was all lads from Strat,' he said, as if this were a well-known demographic sub-group and countless sociological studies had been written about teenage life in Long Stratton. 'Come the last day of the harvest, there'd be a square of corn left in the field and every wild animal on that farm would be hid up in there. I've come away with ten, twenty of the buggers in my time.'

There was a lot more of this: hare-coursing over the fields; nests of children living in tumbledown cottages beyond officialdom's grasp; the cold winter of 1963 when the Tas Valley villages were cut off for weeks. The Ratcatcher had long, brown fingers, their nails chewed down to the quick. Simon imagined them bent over recently-sprung traps, snapped to summon a whippet, ripping open a pheasant's crop. Returned to reception after the interview was over, he seemed an incongruous figure, a revenant from another world making his presence felt against a backdrop of chrome and plastic. Simon watched him stride purposefully down the asphalt drive, his fluff of white hair dancing in the breeze, until one of the receptionists asked him to sign for several cartons of newly-delivered Styrofoam coffee cups.

As the autumn wore on, the Ratcatcher became a fixture on the station. He appeared on the afternoon show, debating dialect usage with Professor Trunnion. He accompanied the radio car to obscure villages on the lip of the Fens and sat in draughty parish halls listening to teams of handbell-ringers being put through their paces. A reporter from the local newspaper visited him in his cottage out on Blofield Heath and exclaimed over his collection of hand-carved decoy ducks. Mr Ferris approved of the Ratcatcher. Simon suspected that he regarded him in the same way that he regarded books about Norfolk churches or the local football team promenading around the city on an open-top bus whenever they won anything. But Simon and Myfanwy, too, were tapping into heritage. On Sunday afternoons they went on excursions to the North Norfolk wilds, inspected the remains of abandoned Angevin castles, walked round bird reserves crammed with snipe, terns and avocets, all the while talking across each other and not listening and finally communicating in that oblique, contrapuntal cipher they had perfected over the years. 'There are some good places on the south coast,' Myfanwy would say, and he would counter with: 'They're going to be advertising the deputy station manager's job after Christmas.' Eventually they would compromise on the blueness of the sea or the crispness of the day or the extraordinary number of black Labradors you saw at Holkham, but all the while the deeper questions went unanswered.

In all these things, like the rain that lurked behind the pale Norfolk sky, uneasiness simmered. 'Come and have a cup of coffee,' Rossy Boy demanded when they met in the corridor one morning a week before Christmas. If the first unwritten law of Norfolk FM was that you always complimented fellow-professionals on their programmes, then the second was that you always drank cups of coffee when they were offered you. Obediently, Simon followed the Ross-meister out to the café twenty yards along the road from Norfolk FM's asphalt drive where such interactions customarily took place. Rossy Boy stirred his cappuccino zestlessly. In the past few months his star had begun to dwindle. The ratings for his show were in decline and several listeners had complained about the live broadcast from Cromer in which he went along the pier asking any remotely pretty girl how many crabs she had caught.

'I haven't got a chance of this deputy station manager's job, have I?' he lamented at one point.

'Relax, Ross,' Simon said, who had never allowed a genuine liking for most of the people he came across to get in the way of personal ambition. 'You're a shoo-in.'

After that Rossy Boy cheered up a bit and insisted on

standing Simon a piece of chocolate swiss roll. Outside battered cars chugged back and forth in the rain and the masts from the nearby boatyard clustered against the turbid sky. The moment Rossy Boy had to return to his duties the space where the reek of his powerful aftershave still lingered was occupied, rather unexpectedly, by Mr Ferris.

'Nice little place this, isn't it?' he said. He looked even grimmer than usual, infinitely depressed and ground-down. 'Sometimes I have breakfast here on my own before anyone else has arrived. Look, here's an idea. You know you've got the Minister for Agriculture coming in the day after tomorrow? Well, let's have the Ratcatcher on as well. See what a real son of the soil has to say.'

Back at the flat, Simon knew that Myfanwy would be burnishing up her CV in pursuit of a junior lecturer's job that had just come up at the University of Portsmouth. Twenty miles away the seals would be lumbering up and down Winterton Beach. Eagerly, he inclined his head.

⚙

The trouble about Norfolk, Simon thought, two days later, was that it underplayed its hand. It crept up on you unawares, worked by stealth. Its effect was profound, but accidental. You could miss what it had to offer. But then, breaking out of the trees on some back road, looking out over the pinewoods on some far-flung beach, you would find yourself, solitary and chastened, wondering at the enormity of that great wide sky. It was not like anywhere else, he decided, and neither were the people in it, even now when the Norwich backstreets were sprouting Polish grocers and Thetford was full of fruit-pickers from Portugal. The Minister of Agriculture was a short, roly-poly character in a pinstripe suit. Perched alongside, still in his check jacket and brown corduroys, in whose turn-ups, Simon noticed, a small pile of detritus had begun to accumulate, the Ratcatcher looked as spiritually detached from his fellow-guest as it was possible for another human being to be. On the other hand, the Minister and the son of the soil were getting on well. Just now the Ratcatcher was producing more anecdotes from his Norfolk childhood.

'We was all just lads from Strat,' he explained, waving a brown hand for emphasis. His face looked more weather-beaten than ever and the wrinkles were expanding into enormous chevrons. What had the lads from Strat got up to? If they were not exactly rural desperadoes, then they had certainly managed to amuse themselves. To judge from the Ratcatcher's memories, they had poached pheasants, brewed moonshine whisky in illegal stills set up in remote barns and gone rip-roaring into Norwich on the bus on Saturday afternoons.

'Village life, eh?' said the Minister, graciously.

And then, without warning, Simon had his premonition of doom. The cosiness of the studio, the warm air rising from the radiators, the steam from the coffee cups, the slow tick of the clock – all these were a deception. It had been a mistake to bring this old gentleman with the chevroned cheeks in to parley with the Minister of Agriculture, a mistake to encourage this dialogue, a mistake to imagine that this revenant from the woods and fields had anything to say to a portly representative of the modern age.

'As to the immediate situation . . .' the Minister began, in response to Simon's polite question about migrant workers, and then, as if catching the scent of something in the space between them, fell silent.

And Simon watched, fascinated, as the Ratcatcher slid his hand out over the desk, snake-like and insinuating, and pulled the slanting microphone stand away.

⁂

'I don't blame you in the least for what happened,' Mr Ferris said. 'Nobody could have foreseen it.' It was six weeks later and the evening of Mr Ferris's farewell party. Plastic cups charged with cheap sparkling wine, the station's freelance contributors – the bowls correspondent, and the woman from the WI who supplied knitting patterns – wandered hopefully round the knots of guests looking for someone to talk to.

'I mean,' Mr Ferris went on – he was reconciled to early retirement now and in a much better mood – 'who would have known he had such a bee in his bonnet about Brexit or the Syrian refugees?' Simon, seeing that he, alone among the ellipse of faces grouped around Mr Ferris, was being directly appealed to, nodded his head. What had really upset him, he realised, was not the Ratcatcher's anguished shouting into the microphone, or the flung pencils, or the Minister of Agriculture taking refuge behind a filing cabinet, but the look of contempt on the Ratcatcher's face when, a security guard hanging on each arm, they had finally dragged him out of the room.

'You know,' Rossy Boy said, sympathetically – his naturally pale face had taken on a greenish shade in the artificial light – 'I must admit I never listened to him most of the time, but I really miss "This Afternoon's Village."'

Mr Ferris's successor had not yet been appointed, but there was a new deputy station manager, imported from the West Midlands and said to be keen on the younger audience. Professor Trunnion's services had been dispensed with and they had all been instructed to play a lot more pop music.

'Never mind, Simon,' Mr Ferris said, catching the drift of Rossy Boy's intervention. 'You'll be out of here soon. Off to Radio 4, I dare say. You and – Melissa, is it? What's she up to?'

'She's very well,' Simon said, not bothering to correct him or to reveal that Myfanwy, her thesis complete and her many job applications ignored, was currently waitressing at a restaurant in Upper St Giles. Not listening to Mr Ferris any more, or to Rossy Boy, whose stubby fingers were scrabbling at the sleeve of his jacket, he found himself looking round the elongated corridor between the two studios where the party was taking place: at the portraits of the Norfolk FM presenters and the still-unshifted crate of bottled water. His own photograph had been taken five years ago and made him look impossibly young, some schoolboy smuggled into the world of local broadcasting under false pretences. At the back of his mind he had an uncomfortable feeling that the emotional investment he had made in all this far exceeded its probable rewards.

The party was dying down now and people were tossing their empty plastic cups into the wastepaper bins. It would soon be time to go back to the flat and cook something for Myfanwy's supper. Outside the February rain, which had eased off for a moment or two while Mr Ferris was making his farewell speech, came down with a vengeance, and he stood in the cramped and comfortless vestibule, his raincoat half on, scarf not yet wound around his neck, wondering idly where he would most like to be, and deciding, finally, that it was out on the plain, under the wide sky, raging around the Norfolk countryside, alien and ungovernable, somewhere out there in the middle distance with the lads from Strat.

NEW FACTS EMERGE

A T 5 A.M. it was still pitch-dark outside, although there were wild animals scuffling in the garden. She stood in the kitchen, which the electric light had turned raw and baleful, listening to the foxes skirmish, as she chewed a piece of toast and inspected the drawings stuck to the door of the fridge. There were several new ones of her and Andrew depicted as enormous, bony stick-insects, in which, she was puzzled to observe, Drew – a modest 5 feet 8 inches in real life – towered over her, a colossal figure two or three times her size. Was this how the twins regarded them, or did they simply lack a sense of perspective? Here on Christmas Eve several of the pictures had a festive aspect. There was one of Father Christmas on a sled pulled by small, spindly reindeer, and another of a kind of ziggurat of carefully stacked consumer goods – CDs, DVDs, bottles – which she suspected Drew might have had a hand in, captioned DADDY'S XMAS STASH. In reality, Drew was going to get a sanding machine with which, it was fervently hoped, he could get to grips on what remained of the back garage. All other bets were off. 'Why on earth do you have to go in on Christmas Eve?' Drew had asked over supper (fish fingers, smiley-face potatoes, spaghetti hoops) the previous evening, and she had replied, as she had done on the evening before every Christmas Eve for the past three years, ever since she had got the senior audit manager's job, 'Red Ensign Club,' and Drew had nodded in the way that he nodded when told that her mother was coming to stay, or that she intended to spend an evening with her old school friend Melanie Albrighton – an acknowledgment that a giant breezeblock had been shunted across the railway track of his life, which no amount of sweet-talking would ever shift.

It was 5.10 now. Somewhere above her head a child halfway between sleep and wakefulness muttered something, but she steeled herself from clattering upstairs to investigate and console. Drew could deal with that one. As she pushed the front door open and stood under the arc of the security light, breathing in sharp air and fishing for the car keys, a fox went skulking off into the hedge. It was bitterly cold. Six months ago, a week or so after their relocation to the Norfolk-Suffolk border, she might have been exhilarated by this combination of solitude, wildlife and breeze-blown hedgerows. Now she was merely neutral. If you wanted to work in London but live in the country – the real country – you had to get up early. Case closed. Unless, of course, you were Drew, who made documentary films for a living and seemed to be able to come and go as he pleased. She got into the car, switched on the Sufjan Stevens CD and bowled off through the empty, mist-streaked backroads towards Diss station.

The 5.47 to Liverpool Street was all but empty, with only three or four commuters to a carriage and no one at all at the mournful buffet, where she bought a cup of coffee and a protein bar that mostly consisted of sunflower seeds. Worse, her fellow-passengers had the complacent, affable look of people who were not heading to town to work but going there to be taken out for Christmas lunches or go last-minute

shopping in New Bond Street. Drinking the coffee and looking out of the train window, where flat, frost-ridden fields drowsed under the mist, she thought about the Red Ensign Club and the peculiar set of circumstances that led to its annual accounts having to be gone through on the morning before Christmas. In theory Copus & Tenterden was too big a fish to audit such a minnow as the Red Ensign Club, which was a services charity with an annual turnover of not much more than £3 million. On the other hand, the senior partner was a trustee and the Red Ensign's chairman was thought to have a son on the board of Copus & Tenterden's management consulting arm, and so the thing had persisted through the years, long after all the other charity audits had been transferred to two-partner outfits in the London suburbs. Not worth doing in terms of the audit fee, but 'good for the reputation of the firm' as people still said sometimes, even in these cut-throat days when most of the partners who believed in questionable abstracts like 'the reputation of the firm' had been hustled off into early retirement. There were some other things, too, that would have the vast majority of Copus & Tenterden's senior audit managers – that is, the ones who weren't women – jib at having to bring the Red Ensign Club back home to port once a year. One of them was that the charity had some ridiculous administrative structure, with fifty or so regional organisers lobbing in funds to HQ when they felt like it. Another was the peculiar and inconvenient tradition, its origins unknown, of signing off the accounts on Christmas Eve. A third was the personality of the audit partner, Harold Carter FCA.

Slowly the mist began to rise off the fields and, in the manner of some vast topographical jigsaw, the familiar landmarks of the journey slid into place. The vast pools of standing water beyond Stowmarket; the terrible new houses erected outside Ipswich; the Stour Estuary stretching out to sea beyond Manningtree. More people got on the train, but not many, so that even by Colchester the carriages were only a quarter full, and she checked her phone, but it was Christmas Eve and traffic was slow, and the only morning caller seemed to be Melanie Albrighton, who was wondering whether to buy her husband a lawnmower as a last-minute present. Picking the fragments of sunflower seed discreetly out of her teeth, she found that none of the questions that flocked into her mind had anything to do with the work that lay before her – that could look after itself – but were, in fact, narrowly domestic. If she got the 14.00 she could be back home by 4, by which time Drew would have returned from taking the girls to the ice rink at Diss and maybe, in that self-admiring way that characterised his contributions to family life, thought about what they were going to eat. That would leave ample time to jump upon the long, crowded conveyor belt of duty, obligation and surreptitious pleasure: present-wrapping; the crib service and the annual re-watch of Jim Carrey in *The Grinch*.

Buoyed up by this timetable - although, naturally, it depended on the whim of Harold Carter FCA - she strode off the train at Liverpool Street as if it were a catwalk and dived into the chaos of the Circle and District Line. It was not living in London anymore that made the tube so odd, she decided. Six months before the crazy people and the schoolkids jabbering a patois so outlandish that you could scarcely tell what they were talking about had seemed part of the deal. Now they were somehow alien and intrusive, a threat to the seemlier world that went on beyond the curtain of the M25. She got off the tube at Westminster, gave the 50p piece she always had stuffed into the palm of her glove against such requests to an imploring teenager in a beanie hat, marched up the steps and went off through the fine drizzle across Westminster Bridge. Lanfranc House, Copus & Tenterden's head office, immemorially known to its inhabitants as the Dark Tower, reared up on the further side. There was no one much about. The security guards were battened down behind their Perspex window and the footfalls of the half a dozen people in transit to the lifts or making a beeline for the basement washrooms echoed in the air. Christmas Eve. The Red Ensign Club. Harold Carter. On the way up to the sixth floor she texted Drew with the enquiry GIRLS UP YET? but there was no reply. He would be doling out the muesli or quite possibly still asleep.

It was still only 8.40 – a whole four hours since she had dragged herself into consciousness back in Oakham – but of course, that meant nothing. There were people at Copus & Tenterden who commuted in from Poole, Devizes, places even further flung, whose train rides home were spent amid piles of spreadsheets and who told their children bed-time stories over the phone. Set against these herculean feats of endurance, the 5.47 from Diss was the softest of soft options. Her phone pinged and she read EATING SUGAR PUFFS & WATCHING THE RAIN. The girls were not supposed to eat Sugar Puffs. Something would have to be done about this. Meanwhile, the far end of the sixth floor, home to Audit Division Three, was all but deserted. Sometimes she had strange surrealist dreams about the sixth floor, in which rivers of orchids washed over its grey carpets or porpoises swam in and out of the doors of the partners' offices, but here in the stark silence of a winter morning there was only the pale reality of empty desks and the overloud tick of unregarded clocks. She put her bag down on the table of the glorified hutch that accommodated Audit Division Three's four senior managers, switched on her computer and read an email from Human Resources about the firm's new inclusivity policy. There were some paper streamers hung over the secretaries' consoles, but otherwise not much in the way of decoration.

On her way through the few tiny pieces of admin that remained to be completed before commercial life shut down for the holidays, she found herself thinking about Harold Carter FCA and, specifically, the words you might use to describe him. The most obvious one was *old-school*, but that wasn't really accurate any more. Nobody in chartered accountancy these days was properly old-school. The old-school partners, the ones who had zealously rebuked secretaries they saw eating ice creams in the street, who had come into work in bowler hats and carrying monogrammed briefcases, who had ordered audit managers out of the room if a client rang, on grounds of confidentiality, who had recommended receptionists to be dismissed if they disliked the sound of their voices, were all retired now, and busy boring the Rotary clubs of Chertsey and Godalming, and their successors had been forced to accommodate themselves to the modern age. *Aloof*, then? The adjective had promise, no question, but again she felt that it lacked something, could not quite convey the sheer incongruity of the thing it was supposed to describe. Part of it, too, was to do with his name. Nobody these days – well, nobody under 70 – was called Harold, which was reserved for grandfathers and policemen in bygone cop shows. She rapped out another text to Oakham, but there was no reply. They were probably still bingeing on illicit Sugar Puffs. It was 9.25

now and there was nothing for it. She wedged a box file under one arm and her laptop and handbag under the other, then changed her mind and decided to bear them in front of her in a pile like a votive offering to some exacting institutional deity and moved reluctantly off along the corridor.

By now there were one or two people about: audit managers who had let things slide in the pre-Christmas rush; nervous trainees wanting to make a good impression. The door of Harold Carter's office was half open, but she could have inventoried the contents without going inside. They included two massive gun-metal filing cabinets, as big as the Marshall amplifiers you saw at rock concerts, a framed practising certificate dating from the days of Mrs Thatcher's second administration, and a portrait of a woman – presumably Mrs Carter – of quite stultifying dowdiness, which bore a faint resemblance to the portrait of George Eliot that had graced the flap of her 'A' Level copy of Middlemarch. Here inside the room, she realised that her memory had not played her false and this was – dog-faced Mrs Carter excepted – the modern equivalent of an anchorite's cell. The comparison was made all the more pointed by Harold's oddly tonsorial hairstyle, which involved a luxuriant lower slope mutating into stark baldness the higher up his pale crown you proceeded. He was a spare, thin, desiccated character who now, struggling to his feet against the constrictions of desk and chair, looked rather like a marionette jerked by invisible wires.

'Good morning, Susan,' he said, gravely, instantly reminding her of one of the points in his favour, which was a genuine old-world courtesy. What with all the gender awareness courses and what-not these days, there were very few partners left who dared to remark jauntily on how nice you were looking this morning, or, at important meetings where the coffee arrived in a pot, expected you to pour it out. On the other hand, Harold carried his courtesies so far that he scarcely seemed to notice you were a woman at all. She had sometimes wondered what he would do if she leaned back in her chair, threw her head up and started peeling off her stockings *a la* Annette Benning in *The Graduate*. Affect not to notice? Stare out of the window? Tell her not to be so silly? It was difficult to tell.

'Good morning to you, Harold,' she said, determined not to take any nonsense right from the start. 'And a Merry Christmas.'

'Yes indeed,' Harold said, and left the festive greetings at that. 'Now,' he went on, as if far too much time had already been wasted and her presence on his carpet with her box file and her laptop was simply a ruse to squander the firm's valuable resources, 'shall we have a look at these documents?'

Beyond the window and its vista of municipal tower-blocks, the sky was growing denser. Everybody always said that there were two ways of dealing with Harold when it came to signing off accounts. The first was to play an absolutely straight bat. The second was to have everything at your fingertips and to have plans laid out for every possible contingency. As they started going through some of the branch returns, she congratulated herself on having paid close attention to category b), so that when Harold complained that the figures for Uttoxeter must surely have been understated, she was able to reassure him that the main fund-raising event had not been staged until a week after year-end and would have to wait until next time. Nervous underlings were sometimes made yet more anxious by Harold's professional manner on these occasions, which consisted, on the one hand, of a habit of drawing a series of hieroglyphs on an otherwise blank sheet of paper held in the crook of one arm, and, on the other, a tendency to halt the proceedings every so often to offer some general remarks on the principles and practice of chartered accountancy. But she was used to this, and it no longer annoyed her. If Harold wanted to sketch Anglo-Saxon runes or whatever they were on his jotter pad and wax lyrical on the duties of their professional calling, then that was up to him. They had just got onto the question of the Red Ensign's fund-raising activities in Newbury when he stopped, took his round, rimless glasses of his head, rolled the handles in his fingers for a second or two, and said:

'Are you never struck, Susan, by the responsibilities of what it is that we do? Here is this organisation, this . . .' – he searched for a moment for the correct expression, while staring very hard at her handbag – 'band of people, all engaged on thoroughly good work, looking to us, to . . . to *authenticate* their achievements.'

Needless to say, a tape recording of these remarks, broadcast to a room full of Copus & Tenterden's junior staff, would have been met with gales of laughter. But she was too old a hand not to know the necessity of feigning absolute seriousness.

'I am struck by them, Harold. I am struck by them constantly.'

Back on the Norfolk-Suffolk border they would be on the way to the ice rink at Diss by now. Had Harold ever been anywhere near an ice rink? It seemed unlikely, but then some of the partners were dark horses. Tyrrel, who ran the insolvency practice, was supposed to play the clarinet in a trad jazz band. To cover the embarrassment of what she had just said, she shuffled the papers in her hands while Harold stared at her curiously – this was another of his behavioural oddities – as if she was just about to perform some complicated conjuring trick. Here on Christmas Eve, a time when good cheer and solicitousness might have been thought appropriate, he was in one of his finicking, pompous moods.

'May I ask you, Susan' – this was said with an extreme gravity – 'why you joined this profession?'

There was no knowing why he had asked this perfectly absurd question. Nobody in the world of chartered accountancy ever asked anybody else why they had joined it. It was like asking an undertaker if he liked the touch of dead flesh. And behind the question lurked something absolutely un-get-at-able. Had he been impressed by the lie about thinking of her responsibilities? Did he suspect her of some fraudulent imposture? In any case, why had she joined the profession? The answer, she knew, could be found in two words: Melanie Albrighton, who had been in her year at Cambridge, currently taught at a further education college in the East Midlands and might have earned £20,000 per annum. But she could not tell him this. When Harold asked you a pompous question, you could only give him a pompous answer. So she let her face go mock-thoughtful and said, as if she were grateful for being asked:

'You know, Harold, it was because I thought that, in however small a way, I could make a difference. And then, of course, we can't all teach English.'

Somewhere in the depths of her bag, which was an expensive Louis Vuitton affair covered in zips and snaps like Janet Murdstone's in *David Copperfield*, her phone pinged. Outside the sky grew darker still, violet tending to damson. The bit about teaching English had been a mistake. It had set up an opposition that could only redound to her discredit. Harold looked even more monkish and austere, ran his finger down the Red Ensign's balance sheet with astonishing speed and asked a particularly nasty question about the interest on the £200,000 that the Club had in some pathetic building society account. Happily, this was one of the many areas she had mugged up on in advance.

'As you can see, Harold, the treasurer had it transferred into that fixed-term bond.'

'Ah,' said Harold, much louder than anyone else in the world would have pronounced it. 'New facts emerge. What effect will this have on their cash reserves?'

She was about to tell him that you could make three withdrawals a year from this particular fixed-rate bond, and that the Red Ensign's cash reserves would be in no way compromised in times of crisis – not that there ever were any; the organisation had limped on unspectacularly ever since some retired naval officer had founded it in 1947 – but decided not to. Bored with Harold, the Red Ensign Club, Lanfranc House and everything in it, she felt an overwhelming urge to look at her phone.

'You'll have to excuse me for a moment, Harold,' she said, hoicking up her bag and marching out into the corridor. She made a feint for the loo in case, as was perfectly possible, he was monitoring her progress from the door of his office, and then doubled back to her desk. The message was from Drew and showed the girls, bobble-hatted and be-scarfed, venturing onto the ice rink. WISH I WAS THERE she messaged back, took a satsuma out of the bag and ate it staring out over

Lanfranc House's northern side to St Thomas's Hospital and Westminster. A boy she had been at college with, and with whom she had once or twice been to the cinema and once pecked quasi-affectionately on the cheek in King's Parade, had just, at the age of 39, been appointed to the Cabinet. Well, he was welcome to that. Back at the Red Ensign party, she found, to her considerable disgust, that Harold had pushed her own spreadsheets to one side and produced some of his own, as well as several documents from an unknown source which he ceremoniously invited her to inspect, on the grounds that he was worried about forecast income for the next year, together with some footling communications that had been received from the Charity Commissioners. They argued about this for much longer than was necessary, and also about an opinion she had received from one of the tax partners that anyone other than Harold would have assumed to be absolutely cast-iron. Once they had got through that, and Harold's spread-sheets had been returned to their gun-metal filing cabinet, it occurred to her to look at her watch. To her surprise, it was 11.30. The morning was hastening away.

'We really ought to be getting on,' she said, not without a certain briskness, as if Harold were a small child late for a music lesson. 'I have to be out of here by just after 1.'

It was clearly not only the wrong thing to say, but the wrong way to have said it. Harold looked down at his wide roll-top desk with its brass inlays, and then, as if seeking emotional support, at the photograph of the plain, spiritless woman. Somehow, she thought, the twenty-first century had passed him by. He should really have been sitting in a gentleman's club in St James's, being brought unwelcome news about the Suez Crisis.

'But we cannot go on,' he said, 'until we have established a proper fiscal context. And new facts have emerged.'

Each partner at Copus & Tenterden had his, or very occasionally her, pet phrases. Smethwick, the head of Corporate Finance, said 'all reet pet' in a Newcastle accent, irrespective of the gender of the person he was talking to. Her audit group team leader said 'Run that one past me again, will you?' five times a meeting. Harold's was new facts and their emergence. Sometimes they had emerged, sometimes they were emerging and sometimes they were only about to hatch, but each time he said it she had a curious vision of tiny, fluffy animals huddled behind a sofa, noses protruding, testing the air to see if it was safe to come out.

'In my judgment,' Harold went on, 'this requires a much more detailed investigation than we have so far been able to allow ourselves.'

To her horror, and ignoring the precedents established in previous years, she found that he was asking her about the reporting arrangements in the Red Ensign's 50 or so regional centres, which, when you thought about it, was like asking one of the football pundits on the TV to look at the Premier League table and explain how each of the goals registered that afternoon had been scored. It was fishing for information that no auditor could possibly want, or in fact need to possess.

'You can take detail too far, Harold,' she said, thinking that when this was over she would have to abandon the dash to Liberty on Regent Street and get straight back to the station.

'I disagree,' Harold said, with what was almost an attempt at heartiness. 'I disagree. You can never take detail too far.'

There was no way of knowing whether, with his spread-sheets and his queries about cash reserves, and all this other pompous rubbish, he was trying to provoke her or genuinely trying to do his job. All Harold's cards were played close to his chest. They looked at some figures, went over what the Red Ensign's secretary had said in his last email, made pencil-marks and rubbed them out. When Harold had re-corrected a statistic for the second time and the clock had ticked on to 12.30 she said, in what was still a basically humorous tone:

'Harold. Are you doing this deliberately? Is this one of your little jokes?'

Her phone pinged again. They would be back from the ice rink and beginning the present-wrapping, and any sensible parent would have been there with them. Harold looked at her in a rather pained way.

'I am aware,' he said, scratching out another figure and printing a question mark next to it, 'that time is of the essence.' As if on cue, a trolly came rattling down the corridor, pushed by a white-coated member of the catering staff. Silently they watched this deeply resentful factotum plonk down a plate of smoked salmon sandwiches, a flagon of orange juice and a bowl of anaemic-looking fruit on the desk and gloomily depart.

'Harold,' she said, almost angry now, 'I don't want your lunch. I want to get back to my children. I don't want to be rude, but we could have finished this an hour and a half ago.'

Harold unwrapped one of the sandwiches from its cello-phane wrapper, slid it into his mouth and champed on it. She looked out into the corridor which, apart from the retreat-ing trolley, was quite empty. Everyone had gone home. A few flakes of snow were coming in against the high window, which in ordinary circumstances would have given her a feeling of mild, festive elation, but now simply depressed her.

Still, she consented to look at some marks Harold had made in the margin of the latest sheet of paper he had turned up and drank a glass of the orange juice, which had not been properly stirred so that the concentrate had sunk to the bottom.

'I really cannot sign off this document,' Harold said, once he had got the sandwich down, 'in its current state.'

'Yes, you can. It's perfectly all right. The man I had it reviewed by said it was fine. Their finance chap says it's fine. Aren't you being a bit . . .' – she considered and rejected the epithets 'nit-picking', 'obstructive' and 'bloody-minded', and ended up with a less obvious belligerent '. . . pedantic?'

A few years ago, when she had joined the firm, there were still evil old men who pounded their desks and proclaimed that 'the partner is always right.' These days, the staff handbook encouraged what was called a 'meaningful dialogue.' The partner was still right at the end of it, but everybody's conscience was appeased. On the other hand, it had been a mistake – a bad mistake – to call Harold pedantic.

'What I suggest,' Harold said, absolutely impassively, 'is that you take these corrections away and then bring the whole thing back to me when it is in a fit state to be ratified.'

To her considerable surprise, she found herself agreeing to this. It was a quarter past one. She would go back to her desk, whirl through enough changes to placate Harold, add a few cosmetic variations of her own devising, skip Liberty and get the 15.00, which would just possibly enable her to make the crib service. As she stalked back along the corridor, she texted Drew BLASTED HAROLD BEING THE BIGGEST PAIN EVER. Drew had met Harold once at a drinks reception and remarked that Lucian Freud would have found him a congenial subject. Back at her computer, trying to make sense of Harold's addenda, she found herself thinking not of the train ride home, which would be murderous, or of tomorrow's arrangements, which included her parents driving over from Towcester, but of Melanie Albrighton, who had been her tutorial partner and who, although nothing was said, had been profoundly shocked when, three months after graduation, she had taken Copus & Tenterden's shilling, or rather the £18,000 a year that Copus & Tenterden then allowed its graduate trainees, and had gone on being quietly shocked for the next two decades.

But what was wrong, she thought, punching in another half-column of figures, in settling for modest ambitions and bourgeois comfort? The trouble with art, as represented by Melanie Albrighton, was its engrained reluctance to pay the rent. All this reminded her of a boy called Jeremy Smallpiece, who had turned up in the same batch of graduate trainees as herself, slouched around the building with an insouciant air, been seen writing poetry in his lunch hour and then resigned in the most spectacular fashion imaginable by charging into the Director of Human Resources' office and declaring that he could not stay a day longer in the moral cesspool that was Lanfranc House. At the time she had been rather impressed by this gesture. Now she thought it was simple vainglory. And what, if it came to that, had happened to Jeremy Smallpiece? Had he actually published any of his wretched poems? No, he bloody hadn't. Much better to settle for bourgeois comfort, she thought, with a regretful glance at that lost and so easily forfeited world of bluestocking fervour.

Half an hour later, almost sprinting back to Harold's office, with her coat over her arm, such was her anxiety to be off, she found, to her vast surprise, that it was empty. The plates and cutlery were still there, and Harold's spreadsheets had been extracted from their filing cabinet once more and strewn all over the desk top, but of the man himself there was no sign. She put the print-outs from her computer next to the spreadsheets and stood there wondering what to do. She decided that she would give him five minutes and then go. The five minutes, during which she stared at the latest set of updates from the Institute of Chartered Accountancy in England and Wales that were lying grimly in the out-tray, soon passed, after which she decided that she would give him another three minutes. As the third of these minutes ticked to a close, and she was standing in the doorway glaring at the empty corridor, Harold appeared at its further end, an intent, purposeful figure walking slowly towards her.

'Here are your corrections Harold,' she said as he came level with her, waving the sheets of paper under his nose and then almost thrusting them into his hand. 'I'm going now. Merry Christmas.'

'But you can't,' he said, in the mystified voice of some ancient sage whose prophesy of blue skies and gentle breezes has just been answered by a plague of frogs. 'You can't. I absolutely forbid it.'

'Sorry, Harold.' She was a yard or two away from him now, her heels jagging into the carpet. This had gone far enough. 'I have to get back to Liverpool Street. My children are expecting me. See you in the New Year.'

'I absolutely forbid it,' Harold said again, the first two words coming out in a sibilant hiss, the second two rising to an outright shriek. He was at her side now, blinking furiously and making little battering motions with his hands, which, though feeble in the extreme, were still battering motions. She had sometimes read articles in magazines by women writers she admired and, in a certain sense, would have liked to be, which told of their self-consciousness and their shame in the presence of men. Those women had never worked at Copus & Tenterden. Three of Harold's bony fingers had locked round her elbow now. She brushed them away and then, for good measure, shot out her own hand and caught him a good one on the point of his beaky nose. This had clearly been the right thing to do, as Harold stopped dead in the middle of the corridor, one hand staunching the blood, which now began to trickle onto his white shirt-front, and she was able to get out her phone, call Security and instruct them to send someone up to the sixth floor as soon as they possibly could.

In the event, the business took several hours to conclude. To begin with they – 'they' being Harold, his head in his hands, the two security guards who had apprehended him, one of whom he had kicked in the knee, and herself – had sat in the Head of Security' office next to main reception. Then the last member of the Human Resources department still in the building was summoned to take statements. Finally, as Harold was not prepared to say anything other than that his wife was expecting him, medical assistance was summoned and she was allowed to go. Standing in the foyer of Lanfranc House, where there were still occasional snowflakes coming in from the river, she noticed that there were one or two drops of blood from Harold's nose on the toe of her shoe, so she wiped them off with a handkerchief.

London was closing down. Most of the office workers had

gone home and the tube was emptying fast. Rattling around the Circle Line and remembering the women in the magazines who wrote about their self-consciousness or their shame, she thought of all the women she had at one point or another in her life wanted to be: the novelist in her book-lined room; the don in her study; Siouxsie Sioux; Bjork. But these were airy phantoms: Melanie Albrighton was welcome to them. At Liverpool Street the concourse was nearly deserted; the last train had gone and the minicab firm whose number she retrieved from her bag wanted £200 to take her back to Oakley. The car could stay at Diss. In the cab she stared out at the East End streets, which were fill of black plastic refuse sacks and the lit-up frontages of kebab shops and mobile phone franchises.

'You have nice day?' asked the cab driver, who might have been Albanian, or possibly Turkish.

'No,' she said. 'Not at all. The worst day ever. But thank you for asking.'

As they swung onto the M25 the phone rang. 'Where have you been, Mummy?'

'Oh Lu, I had to stay at work longer than I thought. Tell Daddy I'm really sorry.'

'But why did you have to stay?' Lucinda persisted.

'There was a silly man who was behaving ridiculously. Did you enjoy the crib service?'

'Yes, I did. I enjoyed it *a lot*. Will you be home soon?'

'Yes, I will.'

The taxi sped down the M25, gliding over the wet tarmac like a swan of steel. Nearer at hand, beneath a blanket of pitch-black sky, the Essex villages slept. Already her mind had moved on from Harold and his clutching fingers and the Red

Ensign Club to the contingencies of tomorrow. Drew could get up and put the turkey in the oven. It was the least he could do. When they hit the M11 she fell asleep, and woke to find the signs pointing to Mildenhall and Thetford Forest. Sometime on Boxing Day, she knew – it was a regular thing with them – Melanie Albrighton would ring for one of her confidential chats, and, not unwillingly, she would attend to the latest instalment of her battles with her students, her husband and the small publishing firm that had been just about to bring out her novel for the past two years. But she could cope with this, she thought, just as, when it came to it, she had been able to cope with Harold Carter FCA in his anchorite's cell. You rode with the punches, concocted your own stratagems and lived to fight again. Paying off the taxi in the drive, watching its tail lights swing away into the gloom of the road beyond, she felt suddenly gripped by purpose and resolve. The front door opened as she came up to it, and she stepped inside, hopeful and expectant, already consoled by the prospect of the new facts that were about to emerge.

IN BRECKLAND WILDS

H ECKY KNOCK HAD lived in the Breckland all his life: in Watton, Methwold, Swaffham and half a dozen other small and inconspicuous places. His father, Sampson Knock, had owned a kale and currant farm on the west side of Garboldisham, but the old man had taken early to drink and died in what to that part of the county was still known as the inebriates' home. As Hecky and his dad had never got on, and as, in addition, old Mr Knock, when not drunk or quarrelsome, had possessed original ideas, Hecky's mother had inherited the farm. But men wouldn't work for a woman in those days and Mrs Knock, who had taken no interest in the four-dozen acres bequeathed to her while her husband lived wasn't about to start now. The farm, consequently, died by inches, most of the kale crop was beyond selling and the blackcurrants, which had once supplied the local supermarkets, were grubbed up for jam. Once his mother, too, was dead, Hecky, devoid of sentiment in this and every other matter, sold it to an agribusiness, gave a fifth of the proceeds to his younger sister, took the money that remained and retired to a cottage six miles away. He was a circumspect man and resolved to live frugally, only digging into the capital to buy necessary things, such as the big chest freezer in which he stowed game shot in the farmers' fields, and the tiny car in which, now and again, he went out cruising the back lanes and, if the paths allowed it, away across the sandy heaths.

When he went driving, shotgun rattling in the boot, a mess

of blankets and old shopping bags staining the back seat, it was to see how things had changed: a meadow with a strew of houses rising over the once unspoilt hill; another cluster of sale signs in a village opening up to colonists. Hecky disliked the new people moving in – Home Counties refugees who commuted from Diss or Thetford on the train and thought they contributed to village life by attending the parish hall panto at Christmas and ordering papers at the newsagent while bringing in contractors to tile their roofs and re-lay their gardens. If Hecky, driving past a house in the throes of refurbishment, saw a builder's van he didn't recognise or a glazier's with London plates, he would hoot in derision, while acknowledging as he did so the futility of the gesture. His sister, Tilda, who did cleaning work for incomers, tidied up their remodelled drawing rooms and walked their nervous metropolitan dogs, was more forgiving. 'There is a whole lot of money to be took there, Heck, and I'd be a fool to turn it away.' There were ten years between them, not to mention the unequal share of the farm, and Heck, nearing sixty now and set in his ways, put it down to the foolishness of youth.

Still, in all of this there were places he cared to go and opportunities he cared to muse upon, sundry twitches on the ancestral thread. He was sitting in one of the Swaffham antique parlours – one that came with a coffee lounge attached, so that the tables melded into the piles of bric-a-brac and the racks of old sheeting – when a woman ten feet distant nodded at him in a meaningful way and he found himself nodding back.

'Know you,' he said, in what was half a question and half a statement.

'Should think you do,' she offered, head cocked and with a fine show of mock-offended dignity. 'Use ta come round the house – your dad's farm – when I was a girl. Carrie Ives my name was then.'

So that was why her gaze had settled on him. He recalled a thin, well-nigh starveling girl who had been cruel to the cats, chasing them and seizing their tails. Her father had sold Mr Knock fertiliser or liquid manure; he couldn't remember which.

'Wouldn't have recognised you,' he said gallantly, noting that Carrie, like her put-upon mother, had run to fat.

'Here, Carl!' she commanded, and the tall, gormless-looking boy, who had been browsing the boxes of old war medals and folded Confederate flags on the other side of the parlour, came shambling by. 'This here's my boy Carl,' she explained as the apparition stood before them, shuffling his feet and breathing a bit too heavily for the exertion involved. 'You say hello to Mr Knock.' Hecky could have done without Carl, and he could have done without Carrie weighing twelve stone and having scarlet dye in what he remembered as ash-blonde hair, but it was nice to meet someone you knew, or had known, here in a world where so much was novel and outlandish, and they spent a comfortable hour boozing tea, turning over the antiques and talking about Carrie's ex-husband, Don, now somewhere in Lincolnshire. Coming back to the cottage at dusk, Hecky found an unlooked-for enthusiasm welling up in him and searched for some way to register its impact. Mrs Knock had left little behind her, but there was an old tureen from the Crown Derby dinner service someone had given her on her marriage to Hecky's dad and he ate his soup out of it, sitting in the half-light of the uncurtained front room with the TV on low in the corner and the occasional car going past in the road outside.

They had a kind of half-arrangement to meet the following week. It was raining so hard as to deter all but a couple of elderly ladies in Inverness capes from Swaffham High Street, but turning up at the antiques parlour Hecky found them – for some reason he hadn't expected Carl – already ensconced over the gingham tablecloth with a meringue apiece. 'Thought you wasn't coming,' Carrie said cheerfully. 'Carl. You go and get Mr Knock a cup of tea.' She pronounced it in the old-fashioned way he remembered from half a century before. *Yew goo an' git.* He liked the fact that she called him 'Mr Knock', which both preserved the social distinctions of 40 years ago and suggested that even now he was a person of consequence, and he liked the deferential look on Carl's blunt face as he plonked the teacup down in front of him. When the rain eased off they got in the car and drove out along the B-roads, where partridges burst crazily out of the hedges and the tarmac was spotted with fresh road-kill. Carl stared blankly out of the windows, seeming not to take things in, but later took a keen interest in his mobile phone. Hecky wondered if he was as dim as he looked. Subsequent discussion established that Carl was all of 22, a 'good boy,' Carrie volunteered, but 'frightened of things.' Hecky suspected that one of the things Carl was frightened of was his mother, but kept that to himself.

Meanwhile, like some frantic, unsubduable dog, the present was still tearing at his heels. They were building a close of new bungalows – terrible things in grey stucco – in the field at the bottom of his lane, and he could hear the snarl of the diggers ripping up the bright green turf. His picturesque cottage was already a draw for estate agents, who sometimes put entreating circulars through his letter box, but now came a neatly-suited man in a Range Rover, who absolutely knocked on his front door, invited him to name his price and offered him cash down. Hecky shut the door in his face, and then, re-opening it as the Range Rover moved off, and thinking that he divined contempt in the man's sleek voice, shouted 'Remainer cunt!' and bent for a handful of gravel to throw.

That brought a policeman from the station at Swaffham, Constable Sharrat, whom Hecky had known and drunk with for thirty years, now turned anguished and reproving. 'Hecky, you can't go shouting abuse at people who want to buy your place. Nor go throwing stones at them neither.'

'He come here again it'll be more than a stone.'

'And another thing. You got a licence for that twelve-bore I see in the hall?'

'I'm working on it,' Hecky told him.

It also brought a visit from Tilda, anxious about the arrival of the police but also alarmed by rumours of his burgeoning social life. 'Hecky, you don't want to be spending time with Carrie Ives that was. Them Iveses were always trouble and you know it.'

'Don't remember them being trouble.' He was surer about the Ives's position in his memory now. 'Just remember old Barty Ives selling dad bags of fertiliser and making out they were friends. Which they was *not*.'

Tilda stared at him. 'Hecky, you don't realise it but you're just a sitting duck. One of these days some fox'll have your leg off and you won't even notice that it's gone.'

'It's just Carrie Ives,' he said, a little bewildered by this onslaught. 'Carrie Ives that used to nip the cat when she thought no one was looking.'

'As for that boy,' Tilda said. 'He ought to be in a home, only she probably can't afford it.'

After that some of the exuberance that had welled up in him when he got out the china tureen and sat watching the cars go by ebbed away. The bungalows were three-quarters built now, and he wandered around the site after the builders were gone for the day marvelling that such desecration could be allowed. If he found a placard with the developers' number on it encouraging people to enquire, he tore it down and left it in the mud. Two Sundays before Christmas, when the village houses were festooned with garish lighting displays of Santa and his reindeer, heavenly angels and fir trees, he and Carrie (and Carl) took lunch in a pub outside Garboldisham. Carl stood at the bar, wedged into a scrum of festive drinkers, and Hecky, thinking to save time, flicked his credit card across to him, saw Carl stare stolidly at it for a moment and then, with surprising dexterity, as if the flourishing of credit cards in crowded rooms was second nature to him, wave it across the rim of the machine. 'That's a good boy,' Carrie told him as he ferried the drinks tray back. 'Say thank you to your Uncle Heck.' Hecky didn't care for the 'Uncle Heck', or the moist tracery left by Carl's fingers on the card, but he was pleased to be informed that Carl was going to his dad's for a week over Christmas.

Ten days later, checking his statement in the hallway of the cottage – it came in the same post as a Christmas card signed 'with every festive good wish from Carrie and Carl' – as builders' lorries raced by in the early-morning gloom, Hecky discovered that someone had helped themselves to a new fridge-freezer and a brace of laptops at his expense. Recalling the day in the pub at Garboldisham, he knew there was only one explanation. He drove over to Carrie's miniature house on the far side of Watton – he had only been there once, and rather enjoyed its unambiguous squalor – just as the street lamps began to go on. The door went unanswered, but the upstairs light was on. There was no one about in the street of shabby houses, so he hauled the shotgun out of the boot of the car and, taking his time, squeezing so slowly on the trigger that the act became almost languid, as if a slowed-down silent film were playing before him, frame by frame, blew out both the downstairs windows and then listened, appreciatively, to the tinkling glass. Driving back along the fog-bound roads, though, he realised that he had made a mistake. It was not Carrie and Carl whom he blamed. The culprit was something wilder and more elemental, something monstrous that had grown to maturity out there in the fields without his sanction. There was no doubt about it, he thought, as he brought the car to rest against the dark verge and stared through the shadows at the newly-built houses as they loomed up behind distant trees: it was the place's fault.

THE BIRDS OF NORFOLK

T HEY WOKE UP in the rented house at Brancaster
just after dawn to find dense orange light bursting in
through the gaps in the curtains. There was an eerie silence
beside and beneath them, which meant that the children were
still asleep, and Mark, sensing opportunity, pushed her head
into the crook of his shoulder and in the insouciant way that,
even after ten years of marriage, she still found slightly shock-
ing, said: 'What are my chances?' But it was only the second
day of the holiday and she was still exhausted and also annoyed
with hm for a variety of reasons she could not quite manage to
separate out, and so she swung her own shoulder well out of
range and said: 'Not the faintest chance. Go and make me a cup
of tea,' and pressed her head back into the pillow. Listening to
him crash down the stairs, as the voices of newly-roused children sounded in his wake, she reflected that anyone presented
with a tape-recording of this exchange would automatically
assume that it was she who held all the trump cards in their
relationship whereas in fact it was the other way around. Still
listening to the racket Mark made as he went about brewing
the tea and the little irritated noises triggered by his exaspera-
tion at not knowing where everything was, she found herself
weighing up points for and against him. On the positive side,
there was the fact that he was actually making the tea, rather
than feigning sleep and bamboozling her into doing it, and also
attending to Josh and Hatty, who were demanding glasses of
milk and biscuits. On the negative was the ping of his mobile

going off – who on earth could he be in communication with at this hour? – and the scheme to move house again, which had been unleashed on her the previous night over what was supposed to be a relaxing supper in a country pub.

Going down the polished pine staircase half an hour later – it was a top-of-the-range let from Norfolk Country Cottages at £2,000 a week – she caught a glimpse of herself in the mirror: small, blonde-haired and discontented and wearing a red and white Breton top that gave her a nautical air. But the sight of the breakfast table, with its neatly-set rows of cutlery and its newly-opened flagon of cranberry juice, was unexpectedly cheering. Even if Mark was one of those men who make an effort largely so that effort may be publicly commended, at least the effort had been made. 'Did you sleep well, Mummy?' Josh asked politely.

'Yes I did,' she lied. 'Did you?'

'Josh cried because he thought there was a ghost in the wardrobe,' Hattie said loftily. 'What are we going to do today?'

'Bird reserve this morning, I think,' Mark said, coming back from the cooker with a plate of French toast and the mobile phone pinging away in the pocket of his khaki shorts. 'Go over to Titchwell and see what's flown in from the Arctic.'

'Daddy says we're going to the bird reserve,' Alice said in a way that she hoped would convey enthusiasm to the children and a mild resentment of decisions made without consultation by Mark. 'But nobody – not anybody – not even Daddy, is leaving this house without putting on a hat and some sun cream.'

'I got some papers ordered from the shop in the village,' said Mark, whom, she noticed, was trying very hard to please.

'They should be here in a minute.'

'That's good,' she said, thinking that she would not have cared if she never saw another newspaper in her life, only for Josh to shatter a tumbler by dropping it on the floor, where-upon the thought of what might have prompted this sudden access of solicitude drifted away from her, flew up into the room to settle among the prints of Norfolk shorelines and whirling gulls and prowling avocets, and the real business of the morning slowly took shape beneath her grasp.

※

'Birds,' Mark was saying in a high, sing-song voice for the children's benefit as they headed north along the coast road. 'Herons and oystercatchers and hoopoes and black-backed gulls.' Alice always wondered if his enthusiasm for the avian fauna of the east coast was quite as serious as he maintained, or simply put on when the occasion suited, like the fleeting interest in international rugby which mysteriously vanished once the Six Nations was over. She was still cross about last night's conversation, and even crosser about the psychological stirrings that lay behind it. Did Mark really want to move house again, a bare two years after they had established them-selves at Richmond, or was it because the bank had given him another bonus - £117, 322 according to Mark's precise calcula-tion - and he couldn't think what to do with it? However much magnified, it was the same motivation that, a decade and a half before, whenever the art gallery in which she worked had given her a tiny pay-rise, had sent her flying into one of the Jermyn Street boutiques to buy a cheap bracelet.

'Oh, and by the way,' Mark said, dropping his Mickey

Mouse on helium voice to include her in the dialogue. 'Apparently the Taverners are here this week. I had a text from Freddie. He says why don't we go round for a drink this evening?'

She considered this for a moment as the breeze blew in from the sea to buffet the side of the car and a stream of ladybirds flung themselves despairingly against the windscreen. 'I thought you said they always went to Limoges these days?'

'Oh, Freddie thinks nobody in France wants to look an Englishman in the eye after Brexit. He says Emma's looking forward to seeing you again.'

'Well we must go then,' Alice said, who knew her social obligations. On the other hand, she had to concede that of all the friends of Mark's introduced to her over the past ten years, Freddie, who worked in some stratospheric level of corporate finance, and Emma, who appeared to do nothing except sit in their big house in Hampstead snipping articles out of *Homes and Gardens*, were by far the most tedious. Worse, there was some secret compact between Mark and Emma that went back before this and occasionally expressed itself in anecdotes about people known at Oxford and the memory of saunters across summer lawns. But she was dutiful girl at heart, so she smoothed her palms against the midriff of her Breton top, ruffled Josh's turbulent hair, told Hattie that granny was expecting a postcard and said how nice, how very nice, it would be to see Emma again.

❦

And in the end the bird reserve at Titchwell turned out to be just what the doctor ordered. While the children, under

Mark's benign supervision, sat meekly in hides inspecting terns and sandpipers and varieties of intruding gulls – there were people round here who were capable of correcting you when you said 'sea gull' and insisting that you should say 'herring gull' – she browsed the gift shop, bought several tea towels and a jigsaw puzzle for her god-daughter's birthday, drank two cups of quite palatable tea and sent a text to the literary agency for which she worked in a part-time capacity. She was back in the gift shop, worrying whether the jigsaw was a bit too complicated for its beneficiary, when the three of them breezed in to find her.

'Did you have a lovely time?' she asked, seeing that Josh looked a bit down in the mouth.

'Yes, I did. I saw a snipe. Only Daddy said it wasn't a snipe.'

'*Definitely* not a snipe,' Mark said, looking into the space behind them and betraying by the redness of his face that he had ignored the instructions about sun cream. 'Hey,' he said, one eye fixed on a protruding bookshelf, 'you can get me that for my birthday if you like.'

In fact, his birthday had been three weeks ago, but Alice knew a hint when it was thrown at her. She paid for the book, a stout, illustrated paperback called *The Birds of Norfolk*, at the till and came back to find the three of them positioned in what she always thought were their most characteristic attitudes: Mark looking about expectantly as if to see what new treat was about to swing into view to entertain him; Josh seeming nervous and put-upon; Hattie examining a pile of toy eagles and felt beachscapes in a faintly calculating away, as if weighing up the chances of her being allowed to buy one.

'Now write in it,' Mark said as she handed the book to him.

And she wrote on the title page *For Mark on his 40th birthday with fond love from Alice,* something which, at this particular moment, with the children offering handfuls of shells for her inspection and the sun flashing off the window frames and talk of the next house removal temporarily in abeyance, was, she thought, as near to the truth as made no difference.

❧

'I saw Georgie Underwood the other day,' Emma said, taking a minuscule sip of wine from her fluted glass.

'Oh did you?' Mark returned, with considerably more animation than Alice remembered him expressing at various comments of her own made earlier in the day. 'What's she up to?'

'Back in Northumberland with that awful man of hers, I should think,' Emma hazarded. 'She said if I saw you I should say "Magdalen Bridge" and you'd know what she meant.'

'Most embarrassing moment of my life,' Mark said cheerfully. The Taverners' house was about as up-market as you could get in this part of Norfolk, with an immense garden and an actual swimming pool in which the children, together with Emma's son Hector, were now gladly disporting themselves. Freddie, who most people thought horribly dull until they were told that he earned £400k a year, was trying to get the cork out of a bottle of Chablis that Alice could see from the label was far more expensive than anything she had drunk in her life.

'Now I,' Mark said, not wanting to be left out of these news updates from the world of bygone Oxford, 'saw Harry Crichton the other day.'

'No? Is he still with that dreadful Camilla woman?'

If these exchanges came close to caricature, then it was because they were meant to. Mark and Emma nearly always upped the conversational ante, as if daring everyone present to chide them for being moneyed, self-absorbed and upper-middle-class twits. What would they start talking about next, Alice wondered, who was dying to get back to the batch of typescripts that the agency had sent her on holiday with. On what tantalising new subject would their shared expertise fall? Over by the swimming pool she could see that neurotic eight-year-old Hector, next to whom Josh seemed a model of well-adjusted self-confidence, was whingeing about something again. The sun was gently declining in the blue, endless sky and she thought how nearly but not quite perfect these kind of days could be.

'Oh you've got that one,' Mark said, plucking the copy of *The Birds of Norfolk* off the none-too-crowded bookshelf.

'It's terribly good, isn't it?' Emma said. 'I always read it when we're here.' The book's cover had a suspiciously pristine appearance, as if it had never been opened, but Alice decided to keep quiet about this. Freddie, who seemed practically to have ruptured himself in extracting the cork, advanced on them with the fresh bottle of Chablis and began to top up people's glasses whether they had asked him to or not.

'Amazing, isn't it,' Mark said. 'The things that turn up here. You know, rare species that have blown off course into somebody's garden in Brundall or somewhere.'

'That's right,' Emma chimed. 'You know, you wouldn't believe it but they once found a golden eagle flying around here.'

Hattie and Josh had had enough of Hector and were

splashing water over him. Pretty soon he would come howling to his parents. Serve him right, Alice thought, unkindly. 'No they didn't,' she found herself saying.

'Oh but they did, Allie,' Emma thoughtfully corrected her. 'I've read about it.'

'No, they didn't,' Alice insisted. She was annoyed not only by Emma's usual omniscience, but by a whole lot of other things: dim, weak-wristed Freddie and his whingeing son; Mark and his secret texting; the bloody new house. 'Some Victorian gamekeeper might have found one rotting on a salt marsh after it came down from Scotland and died of exhaustion, but that's as far as it goes.'

If Mark sometimes shied away from uncomfortable truths, then he was usually prepared to back Alice when the chips were down. So it was he who opened the book and read out under the entry for *Golden Eagle*: 'One, probably an adult male, was found long dead on the salt marshes at Stiffkey in November 1868 and is the sole record for Norfolk.'

Shortly afterwards a snivelling Hector arrived on the terrace clutching his wrist in an odd way, and Freddie, suspecting a fracture, volunteered to drive him to the A&E department at King's Lynn.

⁂

Later, back at Brancaster, as the children lay somnolent in front of the TV and the shadows of the apple trees made fantastic patterns over the garden, she sat at the kitchen table reading one of the manuscripts the agency had sent and watching Mark roaming around in the twilight talking into his mobile. *The Birds of Norfolk*, with its tender inscription, sat next to her coffee cup. Sometimes, she thought, the small victories were the best. She darted another glance at Mark, whose be-shorted knees were glinting in the pale light, wondered who it was he was talking to, and, remembering the pained expression on Emma's face, was surprised to discover how little she cared.

SUNDAY WITH
THE BEARS

H E   W A S   L E S S skilled at piloting a car than she had expected, and so the journey was into its third hour by the time he parked up on the verge a mile or two north of Aylsham and admitted that they really were lost. These were the days before Satnav and smartphones, so they got out of the ancient but still stylish Saab, and stared rather desperately at the AA map of North Norfolk, which Susie held pinioned on the bonnet. She suspected that James, who worked on the arts desk of a national newspaper, was puzzled by things like cars, maps and petrol stations and that however fundamental to the smart, urban lifestyle he aimed to pursue, they were thoroughly inimical to the person who lurked inside him. In the end the map was no help and it took a call from a phone box placed incongruously between two cornfields to set them right. In the distance the last of the morning's clouds had drifted away and there were flocks of black birds moving in and out of distant fields. They drove cautiously on into the sun, past the incoming traffic of minibuses, motorcycle convoys and fleets of cyclists heading towards Norwich and then into a labyrinth of back lanes. Here, once again, the sheer oddity of the task they were bent upon stole up on her and she reached out a forefinger and tapped the nearer of James's wheel-bound hands.

'Who exactly are the Bears?'

He was a tall, thin boy with ash-blond hair who looked and sounded as if he ought to have been to an ancient public school but mysteriously had not. On the other hand, the arts desk was apparently full of modern-day versions of Sebastian Flyte, so perhaps some of their influence had worn off on him. Keeping his eye on the approaching tarmac, which was full of fresh road-kill, he said: 'A very distinguished group of old gentlemen.'

'How many is a group, exactly?'

There was a dead muntjac sprawled in the road twenty yards away of such prodigious size that he had to swerve round it. 'Three, I should think. Unless they've got somebody staying.'

'But what are they distinguished for?' She knew she was letting herself in for trouble with this question, and that the levelling of it would expose degrees of arts-world ignorance that might come back to haunt her. At the same time, she was suspicious of the blanket of admiration flung over every subject to which James turned his hand. There must be un-distinguished writers of novels out there, and second-rate painters and useless ceramicists, only James seemed never to have come across them.

The dead muntjac was thirty yards behind them now, a bloody hump in the ever-narrowing road. There had been no signposts for the past mile and a half.

'Well now,' James said, who she could tell was trying hard not to patronise her and to whom she was half-grateful for this indulgence and half-annoyed that there should be any hint of patronage in the first place. 'There was that Channel 4 documentary about them a couple of years ago. And then Frankie's last novel caused quite a stir.'

Susie, who worked for an aggressively lowbrow publisher at whose editorial meetings Frankie's novel would have been regarded as the airiest arty nonsense, had a feeling that 'caused quite a stir' meant 'got reviewed in the *Times Literary Supplement*, but she listened obediently as the Saab bowled on and the encroaching plant life hung dangerously over the windscreen and the insects rampaged in and out of the wound-down windows. By the time they got back on the coast road – it was 11.30 and she was bursting to go to the loo – she had learned that the Bears were nothing less than a cultural phenomenon, that they had lived, or at any rate weekended in their Norfolk fastness for upwards of thirty years, that they were supposed to operate a 'salon', and had mixed on more or less equal terms with E. M. Forster, W. H. Auden and Sir John Betjeman. 'Queer as coots,' James had added, in case there should be any doubt as to why three elderly men of artistic tastes might want to share a house in North Norfolk, secluded from the public gaze. As the lecture – which was not quite a lecture, as there was room for questions and occasional detours – went on, she conceded that they were at a stage in their relationship where this forced march over four counties to visit three old men she had never met in their rustic lair still seemed a highly desirable way of passing the time, and that if James had proposed a jaunt to a sewage farm or a children's spelling bee she would have regarded it as a gift from providence.

The sun grew hotter by the minute, the air rushed in through the open windows, James gave one of those secretive, unfathomable smiles that were such a vital part of his emotional repertoire, and there they were, finally, in Wiveton, with its seemly greensward, its ancient stone and, miraculously, just where James had claimed it would be, a gate in the middle of a long, low fence marked 'The Old Rectory.' As they laboured up the gravel path, through the wide, neatly tended garden, she tried to comprehend the edifice that rose before her, with its descending planes of blistered thatch and white stucco frontages, and decided that it was something more than a large cottage and something less than a *bona fide* country house. She was just wondering who cleaned its substantial interior and who did its cooking and washed its sheets, when they arrived at the front door. 'They must be in the garden,' James deduced, after several rings had gone unanswered – he sounded huffy, as if only a reception committee with lofted flags could have soothed the discomfort of the past half-hour. And so they followed a meandering stone path that led round the side of the house, and made a detour through a kitchen garden where lettuce beds drowsed under fine netting. There was a spade stuck firmly in the newly-watered soil and the resemblance to a Beatrix Potter illustration was so uncanny that you half expected to find Mr McGregor abducting the Flopsy Bunnies in a sack. Finally they came to a limestone terrace above a verdant lawn dotted with croquet hoops.

Here, talking animatedly, beneath a high canvas awning hung between two red and white poles, in deckchairs, dressed near-identically in whitish linen suits and open-necked shirts, sat three elderly gentlemen, one of whom was waving a pink hand in the air to emphasize a conversational point. As social embarrassments went it was not quite the worst thing she had ever experienced, and yet, as she was forced to admit, it came pretty close to the moment when she and an undergraduate boyfriend called Stuart had turned up at his parents' house in Godalming to find the pair of them and another free-and-easy couple playing strip poker in the drawing room. What made their arrival on the terrace beside the canvas awning and an occasional table laid out with tiny bone-china tea cups so embarrassing was the solidarity of the audience. To begin with there was the way in which the three old gentlemen carried on talking to each other even when she and James were plainly in view. Then there was the way in which, as at some secret signal, they simultaneously stopped talking and sat primly regarding her, as if nothing she could possibly say would excuse this interruption and that countless tribes of august females – queens, empresses, dowager duchesses and the principals of women's colleges – had tried and failed before her. Finally, there was the rather plaintive way in which James, who had caught the scent of her own terror, said: 'This is Susie. I hope you don't mind my bringing her over to see you.' Oddly enough, this seemed to be the right thing to have said, as the oldest and smallest of the old men all but simpered and muttered something about 'absolutely adoring pretty girls.' Their hauteur cast to the winds, the Bears – if indeed these were they – fell over themselves to offer hospitality.

'The young lady must take a cup of tea,' the second of them chipped in.

'But she will have to take us as she finds us,' warned the third.

And so they sat on the limestone terrace and drank weak China tea out of the tiny cups – which of all the beverages available on a sultry summer morning in late July Susie thought was probably the most unsuitable of all. A jay screeched in the tree tops, a tabby cat mooched sullenly out of the house and lay flexing its extremities on the lawn, and she wondered what Mr Savage, her boss at the publishing firm, who had once sponsored a book called *Sex Tips for the Over Sixties*, would think of her, and the Bears, and the Old Rectory, Wiveton, and the new, or rather the very old, world in which she had inexplicably fetched up.

⁂

'Wasn't it Morgan who said that the higher you went up the mountainside the harder it was to tell the sheep from the goats?'

'No it wasn't. It was Sligger Urquhart.'

'I was always told that you should either call him 'Sligger' or 'Urquhart', not 'Sligger Urquhart.''

Susie supposed that 'Morgan', who had wandered into the conversation once or twice before and then wandered out of it again, leaving no very great impression of his talents or personal resonance, was E. M. Forster, but she had no idea who Sligger Urquhart was, what highly important things he had done or what sparkling promontory of the world he had occupied to the satisfaction of those around him. Ninety minutes had passed, and they were about three-quarters of the way through lunch, which the Bears, with no self-consciousness whatever, called 'luncheon.' So far this repast had consisted of a thoroughly nasty soup, apparently made of dilute soap and twig-fragments, over which everyone except herself had pleasurably exclaimed, and a fanciful chicken-and-rice affair, which had no flavour at all, although someone named Frances had reportedly approved it on her last visit. Just now they were champing away at some sickly meringues with so much cream oozing out of them that you needed to keep a napkin handy to wipe the overflow off your chin. On the other hand, sitting with the Bears around their worryingly ornate dining table was preferable to being asked to identify some of the people in the immense montage of photographs framed under glass on the far wall, this being the activity that had occupied them for the half-hour before lunch – luncheon – began. The only consolation had been that James seemed to be almost as bad at it as she was and had confused Peter Pears with Benjamin Britten.

'Wasn't Sligger Evelyn Waugh's tutor at Oxford?' James said, who was clearly desperate to make up lost ground.

'Not at all,' Frankie said. 'Evelyn was at Hertford.'

By this stage she was beginning to get the hang of the different, and in some cases contending personalities on display. Frankie, he whose novel had caused such a stir, was the oldest and smallest, so frail and diminished beneath the weight of his linen suit that he sometimes seemed ready to topple over onto the carpet. Basil, taller and slightly younger, was thought to write, or perhaps only to have written, a weekly column about classical music for the *New Statesman*. Ralph, of conventional size with a drooping eyelid and a carbuncle the shape of a water chestnut on his damson-coloured cheek, had been represented as 'toiling away for years' at a biography of someone whose name she had failed to catch. Somehow, though, these individual characteristics were as nothing when compared to the collective front the Bears presented to the world as a whole. For a start, there was their rampant juvenility. Basically, they all behaved as if they were about 12, gave little shrieks of laughter if anything amused them and actually said 'tee-hee' like the characters in children's books. Item two was their unabashed ignorance of contemporary culture. They had heard of Mrs Thatcher (whom they disliked), but the Live Aid concert that had been on TV a fortnight ago had somehow escaped them. Item three, in some ways even more annoying than the other two, was the constant nit-picking. There had already been one quite serious argument about the exact height of Charles I, which had seen Frankie haring off to the library to check in the *Oxford DNB*.

'And when do you expect to finish?' James was asking Ralph, presumably of the project on which he had been toiling away for years.

'It's all very difficult,' Ralph said abjectly, but not quite so abjectly as to make it sound as difficult as all that. 'You see, Sylvia promised me the papers and then the poor girl went and died and I've an awful feeling that her daughter sold them to some *collector*.'

'If I know Sylvia,' Basil said, coming back into the room with five cups of coffee on a gnarled wooden tray, 'she was quite capable of selling them to a collector herself. You remember how badly she let Raymond down with that book he was writing about Leslie Stephen.'

His voice, which was high and querulous, floated off into the ether to mingle with the buzz of the bees from beyond the window and the curious little whimpering noises that Frankie made in the ordinary course of picking up tea spoons and putting them down again. Over the coffee, which was bitter and could have done with a lot more sugar than the amount provided, she realised that she was beginning to revise her opinion of the Bears. For about half an hour after her arrival she had simply assumed that they disliked her, resented her presence in their hideaway and wished her gone. Now she had an idea that, according to their very limited lights they were doing their best, and that the creaking smiles and the offer of abstruse condiments – there was some terrible sauce that they put on the chicken – were genuinely meant. This feeling hardened after lunch when Frankie disappeared on some private errand ('I expect he's gone for a snooze. He usually does about now'), Basil drew James out into the garden for some equally private conversation and she found herself volunteering to help Ralph with the washing-up. She had not, hitherto, taken much notice of Ralph, who had had less to say than the others over lunch, but here he was in the Old Rectory's spacious kitchen, pink-faced and, she decided, like some would-be friendly old uncle gone slightly wrong, kitting her out in an absurd, lavishly-pleated apron that came down practically to her knees and had presumably once been worn by an Edwardian scullery-maid.

'I should warn you,' he said, with an absolutely awful gravity and picking up a tea towel about the size of a horse blanket, 'that I'm a copper-bottomed *martinet* about this sort of thing.'

What was this sort of thing? The washing-up? Domestic routine in general? Having to entertain some unknown woman whose boyfriend worked on a newspaper arts desk? It was difficult to tell. She held a couple of wine glasses negligently under the hot tap so that their rims clashed and nearly shattered, was told, with a sharp intake of breath, to be careful, and insisted, rather too loudly, that she was being careful. After that they got on better. Outside on the terrace James and Basil were deep in conversation, or rather Basil was talking implacably while James stood looking uncomfortable with his hands in his pockets.

'Why are you all called the Bears?' she asked, swilling more hot water over the rest of the wine glasses. Unexpectedly,

Ralph brightened up, put down the horse blanket and lost his air of peevishness.

'Oh, it's rather amusing. A friend of ours was staying, years ago. He's dead now. Anyway, we'd said goodbye and he'd gone out to his car, and then Frankie remembered that he'd forgotten to ask him something and dashed out to catch him before he drove off, and he looked up and said "Exit, pursued by a bear" – you know, the stage direction in A *Winter's Tale*. And then we went out to see what was going on, and Frankie said "several bears." And then somebody wrote something in *The Times* diary, and they've been saying it ever since.'

Well, Susie thought, shoving the last of the plates into the drying rack, there were worse nicknames. Some girls she had shared a corridor with at college who had a passion for taking an immensely formalised version of afternoon tea together each day in their best clothes had been known as the Lezzie Friends. With the washing-up at an end and Ralph now embarked on some complex manoeuvre involving the rearrangement of various bits of cutlery in their drawers, she drifted out onto the terrace, where Basil had disappeared and James was standing on his own, one hand massaging the back of his scalp and the other holding an unlit cigarette.

'You could have worn a skirt.'

There was an aeroplane high above them making vapour trails in the otherwise empty sky and she watched it for a moment. Did the Bears ever fly? She could imagine them making a tremendous fuss about baggage checks and getting things out of the overhead lockers.

'If you wanted me to wear a bloody skirt you should have said so.'

'Just joking.' James, so adept at managing the small-talk

of books-world parties or seeming to take an interest in her parents, was not at ease among the Bears and it showed. He reached out and touched the side of her face. 'Look. The paper wants me to go to Brussels next week and cover the Tina Turner gig.'

'I thought the paper only liked Beethoven concerts and the Bolshoi Ballet?'

'It's Live Aid. They didn't realise there were all those young people and that they liked pop music so much. They've decided they have to move with the times. Anyway, I thought you could come to and we could make a weekend of it.'

She was thinking about this, about Brussels in the summer and discreet hotel rooms with half-drawn curtains and the ecstatic figures in bright air rising to greet Tina Turner, when she became aware of Basil's approach onto the terrace, Panama hat perched athwart his curiously egg-shaped head and a wooden mallet in each hand.

'I'm afraid it's a rule of the house that our guests should play,' he said, as if droves of cabinet ministers and foreign potentates had been driven out of Wiveton for omitting to discharge this signal favour to their hosts.

And so the five of them settled down on the mole-haunted lawn to indulge in what Frankie called 'taking a turn at croquet,' a game that Susie was extremely bad at, at which two of the Bears appeared to be cheating horribly, and which ended, at any rate for her, with Ralph jamming his foot on the top of her ball as it rested against his own and gleefully despatching it into the long grass twenty yards away to riotous applause. And that, Susie thought, was how she would remember them: three plump silhouettes caught in the shadow thrown up by the overhang of the trees and the late-afternoon sun. James, standing calmly alongside, looked as if he fitted into this tableau, but in the end did not. He was too young, too presuming, not good enough at catching the cultural cues that were flung at him. The day was wearing on now, and she knew they ought to be getting back – there was a sales conference down at some hotel in Hillingdon the following morning – but James was being shanghaied off by Basil to admire the visitors' book or some such rubbish ('Yes, Iris has stayed here several times, tee-hee') and so, thinking that she could do with a rest from the chatter and the croquet and the meaningful glances that seemed to be fired at her whenever she opened her mouth, she went and took refuge in the kitchen garden, where a giant bank of shadow had reared up over the wooden bench that lay at the further end, and sat there taking her ease.

But whatever hopes she had of solitude were straightaway dashed as there came a dense, arhythmical noise made up of heavy breathing, disturbed foliage and expensively-shod feet treading down gravel, and after a moment or two Frankie emerged out of the bushes and, after a further moment of almost pitiable indecision, came and sat down beside her. Once again, the sense of having wandered into a story by Beatrix Potter was a bit too strong for comfort, for Frankie, she now realised, with his potbelly and the way he peered over the rims of his spectacles, reminded her of the Alderman Ptolemy Tortoise in *The Tale of Jeremy Fisher*. Once seated, he laid a thin, quivering hand on his knees, inspected it anxiously as if he feared it might take on a life of its own and go scuttling away into the lettuce beds, and then said, rather slyly: 'I do like your –' she thought he was going to say 'young man' in the way that her grandmother would have done, but in the end he settled for 'boyfriend.'

'Yes, he's nice isn't he?' She knew that 'nice' was no sort of word at all, and certainly no sort of word for James, but what else could you say?

'I do like the way young men wear their hair these days,' Frankie volunteered, bringing out a second and rather more mottled hand and slapping both of them on alternate knees like a jazz drummer getting into his stride. 'I believe some of them even have it *permed*, you know.'

'I suppose they do.'

She had a certain amount of experience of confidential elderly men: grandparents, benign and otherwise; the belligerent demographic known in the Yorkshire town of her childhood as 'right old bastards'; raddled company chairmen hovering on the brink of retirement. But she had never met anyone like Frankie.

'You see,' Frankie said – he looked terribly unhappy, far more miserable than the thought of young men getting their hair permed ought to have made him – 'he reminds me of a friend of mine.'

'Does he?'

'Yes he does.' There was a faint snuffling noise that she could not account for, until, by degrees, raising her head, which had been trained on Frankie's be-bopping hands, she realised that he had begun to cry. For half a minute neither of them said anything. A tear or two – they were big, glinting things unlike any tears she had ever seen before – coursed down Frankie's wrinkled old face, and she sat there in silence, sympathetic yet stricken, wondering what on earth he was going to say next. High above them a heron was slowly flapping away in the direction of the church tower.

'A very good friend of mine,' Frankie said, a moment or so later. 'A *special* friend, if you see what I mean. But then he died.'

There was nothing for it but to put out her own hand, which Frankie seized and held onto with a gulp of emotion, as if letting go of it would see him instantly tumbled into a huge, fiery pit that burned beneath them. They sat there in silence until James, bursting through the bushes after his stake-out with the visitors' book, came triumphantly to claim her.

಼

They drove back along the A11 in the twilight, with a gigantic seedcake, pressed upon them by Ralph, its begetter, sitting on a polystyrene salver on the back seat. James, respectful to the point of reverence about the Bears and their achievements on the way down, had now turned blasé and faintly contemptuous.

'Sorry to have inflicted all that on you,' he said. 'I had my doubts from the moment they brought in the soup.'

'Oh I didn't mind,' Susie said loyally. She was thinking about tomorrow's sales conference at the horrible hotel at Hillingdon and the equally horrible book about Formula One racing it was her responsibility to present. When this intimidating spectre had passed on its way, she went back to the memory of Frankie sitting on the garden seat with the tears glistening on his withered chin.

'And as for Basil thinking he can walk into that music critic's job on the paper,' James went on.

'I thought you said Basil was a highly distinguished musicologist?'

'So he was, in about 1957. But things have moved on a bit since then.'

Things were always moving on, Susie thought. None of the pleasant inertia that had characterised her teenage years seemed to have accompanied her into her twenties. There were already new paths offering themselves, tantalising prospects that taunted you with the regret you would hoard up for not daring to take them up. Looking at James as he drove on, his insouciant air altogether failing to disguise that he was having to take this chauffeuring of her down the A11 very seriously indeed, she wondered rather forlornly if she had got him wrong, and rather than being the knight in shining armour come to take her away from a life of flat-sharing in Clapham and horrible sales conferences, he was just like every other man she had ever known, which was to say ever so slightly insecure and getting by on self-confidence rather than talent. This posed the question: just what exactly was she getting by on? She had wanted to ask one of the other Bears about Frankie's special friend, but in the end had not dared to, for fear of what demons might have been freed from the vault of memory. The Saab sped on into the dusk and James, who clearly assumed that the day had had no effect on the way in which they regarded each other, or the difficulties that lay ahead, said, a bit grandly:

'So, what about Tina Turner then?'

But her mind was back at the sales conference and *Formula One: A Fan's Guide*, which, whatever might be said against it, was not quite as bad as the football manager's ghost-written autobiography.

'We'll see,' she said, one eye on the knee on which Frankie's quivering hand had briefly alighted, the other fixed on the endless conveyor belt of the rapidly advancing road.

FORTY YEARS

IT HAD STARTED to rain as he came through the stone gates of the cathedral close, and this, together with the gusting wind, meant that all the bright spaces beneath the antique lamps were full of displaced water blowing out into the darker world beyond. Big, expensive cars were lumbering up from the second gate at the close's further end looking for parking spaces under the Nelson statue, and a minibus jammed into one of the reserved bays beneath the school chapel was disgorging men in dinner jackets and black bow ties. Meanwhile, the rest of the close, stretching away into unillumined gravel paths and banks of shadow flung up by the walls of the cathedral hostry, looked like the setting for an M. R. James ghost story. Somewhere in the middle distance there would be satyrs' eyes flashing through the murk or minor canons up to no good. The rain was coming down harder now and some of the men in dinner jackets broke into a shambling jog as they set off. Emboldened by this sense of purpose, the thought that even here, on a December Saturday night, amid wind and rain, there were still protocols that knowledgeable people could sniff out and stick to, he toiled along in their wake. Whatever the embarrassments of the next three hours, somewhere amongst the oblong tables and the willed raucousness there would be order of a kind.

The band of dinner-jacketed joggers had already broken down. They stood uneasily under one of the street lamps, brushing the rain off their faces and stroking plump calves that had begun to feel the strain, gearing themselves up for a second putsch. One of them, unknown to him, said, 'Hello, Richard,' and he gestured amicably back. Twenty yards away, on the triangular patch of asphalt formed by the gates of the playground, the approach to the school car park and the left-hand flank of the cathedral, there were people stealthily commingling, and a man in a kilt with a tartan plaid over his shoulder who looked horribly like Simon Callow in *Four Weddings and a Funeral* was telling the woman standing next to him about his Scottish ancestry. Still, Richard realised, he had not seen anyone he recognised. On the other hand, this was to be expected. The joggers were looming into view again. They had got their second wind now and were in tight formation, like a rugger scrum about to settle down. Not wanting to risk another encounter with the man who had said hello, he pressed on into the school car park, where the ramparts of the bishop's palace stood gleaming beneath a a cascade of greenish light and a security guard in a hi-vis jacket was aimlessly directing people in all kinds of different directions at once.

'Bobby,' a woman's voice said, close at hand. 'Maisie said the Baxter twins were coming. Isn't that good?' He wondered who the Baxter twins were and what was so good about their reconvening. The school had gone mixed-sex in the 1990s, long after he had said goodbye to it. His own children had reported that the girls had been a civilising influence. Well, he was all in favour of civilising influences. He had a vision of girls in stiff, formal tunics like the ones in the St Trinian's films, handing out cups of tea and rebuking the foul language of their beetle-browed consorts. Five yards behind him, the man in the kilt was clearly having trouble persuading anyone that he came from Kirkcudbrightshire. Fifty yards in front of him the refectory loomed out of the night sky, lights blazing from its serried plate-glass windows, like an ocean liner becalmed in a sea of blue-black ink, and he became aware, as he always did on these occasions, of a feeling of mingled familiarity and unease. Here there would be chartered accountants and solicitors and land agents, hospital consultants, quantity surveyors and the lessors of residential property, the local professional classes, red in tooth and claw. Here, too, would be blasts from the past, icy winds sweeping in across the Norfolk flat, unexpected challenges, tricksy intimations of time past. All this would need the utmost vigilance.

There were some blonde girls in frothy, formal dresses hanging around by the refectory entrance who looked far too young to be at the school, let alone attend one of its reunion dinners. He felt rather than saw the figure in the shadows beyond them, which turned out to be not one of M. R. James's flashing-eyed satyrs but a man called Henry Parkes, who was wearing a transparent plastic mackintosh over his evening suit and whose hair – sparse at the best of times – was sticking to his forehead in sharply individuated strands. The blonde girls faded away and Henry Parkes, with the oppressed, put-upon air that seemed always to hang over him, stepped out into the lamplight.

'How did you get here?'

'I cycled in, of course.' Henry lived at Loddon, about ten miles out, and had no car. Richard caught the faintly accusatory tone of the 'of course.'

'How's Yolande?' Richard asked, making a heroic effort to remember the name of the tall, angular woman festooned with batik jewellery in whose glacial company he had last seen Henry a year and a half ago.

'She's all right, I think,' Henry said mysteriously. His brow creased over for a moment and he beat his thin hands nervously against the hem of the plastic mackintosh. Then, as if anxious to change the subject, he said: 'Do you think my bike will be OK? I forgot to bring a lock, so I left it in that shelter by the playground where they store the sports equipment.'

'Bound to be.' There were more people going by now: younger men snug under golf umbrellas; a retired member of staff or two taking care on the slippery tiles; all of them determined to give Henry a wide berth. Time did odd things to the people you had been at school with. Some of them seemed more or less unchanged. Others were like their original selves only more so. A few were so dramatically altered that they reminded you of those rich people who bought expensive houses only to knock them down and start again from scratch. Henry fell into this third category. Now that his hair had started to go, his bulb of a head looked bigger and more unwieldly, and he had an odd way of pivoting on one leg while keeping the other one poised in mid-air like an anteater's proboscis. But Richard was used to Henry, who could be relied upon to behave adequately if you took him in hand. They hung their coats up in the vestibule, gave their names to a girl with a clipboard and moved on gingerly into the refectory itself.

'Are you still working for that furniture firm at Yarmouth?'

'No,' Henry said, with grim satisfaction, like a hobgoblin inspecting his hobbit traps. 'I pretty soon got out of there, I can tell you.'

'People not OK?'

After university Henry had trained as an accountant, but he had never really acclimatised himself to the profession.

'On the day I left,' he said proudly, 'I stood in the doorway – the manager had come out to see me off – and told them that I'd sooner commit suicide than stay there a moment longer.'

The refectory was a long, low building, rather sticky underfoot, with a couple of dozen tables stretching down to the far end. A few utilitarian Christmas decorations hung here and there, and on the wall between the vestibule and the first serving hatch was a series of group photographs, representing phases in the school's development over the past half-century. Richard steeled himself to inspect the first one and found that some unerring instinct had led him to the 1978 picture. And there they all were, distributed around the back two rows: himself, and Henry, and M. J. Q. Whitmore, captain of the Cricket XI, who was once supposed to have seduced the senior master's daughter on a table in the junior library, and C. J. Mortimer major, who had collected bus tickets in a paper bag as a hobby, and D. S. Proctor-Jones, he of the extensive Swedish pornography collection, and dozens of others, known and unknown. At this remove their hairstyles seemed as remote and fantastical as the chignons of the French Second Empire. To look at them at they stared out of the photograph – by turns hopeful, stolid, anxious, expectant, bored or half-amused – was to get a terrible sense of – what exactly? Life working its purpose out? Promise unfulfilled? Some vast, ineluctable pattern whose real implications were still waiting to make their presence felt? It was difficult to tell. Henry stared resentfully at the photograph, as if he suspected it of being tampered with and half the faces Photoshopped in.

'Shall we go and see where we're sitting?'

Henry did his anteater's proboscis-pivot again and nearly collided with a waitress bearing a tray of Champagne flutes.

All around them ghostly, half-remembered figures went fluttering by. A sandy-haired retired history master whom Richard knew had joined the staff three years after he left came up and said eagerly: 'How nice to see you again. I expect you remember me teaching you Tudors and Stuarts.'

'Yes I do,' Richard said. 'I remember it very well.' Illusions of this kind were better undefiled. If people wanted to think they had swum naked with him in midnight pools or faced down bullies in blood-soaked playgrounds, they were welcome to it. They pressed on down the line of tables, past the impossibly juvenile class of 2017 and the class of 1959 (half a dozen nicely got-up old men with bowties in the school colours) and came at last to a kind of debatable land, not so well lit and to which the refectory's heating system seemed not to extend, given over to the classes of 1978 and 1979. Most of the class of 1979 had already taken their seats, but no one from 1978 seemed yet to have arrived. Richard looked at the place cards and found that he was sitting with Henry on one side of him and none other than M. J. Q. Whitmore on the other. He tried to remember what had happened to M. J. Q. Whitmore and whether or not he had become a solicitor or, as seemed more probable, trained as a dentist. Henry was staring at the cards with an anguished look.

'Don't tell me you've been nurturing a secret passion for Mark Whitmore all these years?'

'Of course I haven't.' Henry had never been very good at irony. 'Do you know who he married?'

'Who was the unfortunate woman?'

A waitress had squeezed into the space between them and was busy arranging knives and forks, but Henry was not easily silenced.

'He married Cecily Mottram. You know, Liz's sister. Liz Mottram.'

Henry was always saying things like this, bringing out little fragments of information from some long-cherished hoard whose significance was completely unintelligible to the people around him. Richard tried to remember who Liz Mottram was and why the fact of her sister Cecily having married Mark Whitmore, the potential dentist, was so important to Henry, however many years after it had happened. The chaplain was saying grace now at a microphone, which had been set up on a mini-podium twenty feet away and they listened to him respectfully. A big burly grey-haired man about three inches taller than anyone else in the room came and sat down next to them, threw out both fists crossways so that he could shake their hands simultaneously and said: 'Hi, I'm Mark Whitmore.'

'We know who you are,' Richard said, who would not have dared to talk to him like this in 1978.

'I'd like you to know,' Whitmore said, in whom some kind of recognition had now dawned, 'that I have forgiven what you wrote about me that time, but I have not forgotten it.'

Several people had said this to Richard over the past thirty years, usually with reference to books of theirs he had reviewed, but never anyone he had been at school with. While he was wondering what to say in return the food came and they set to work on it. The terrine tasted as he imagined an old sock lightly flavoured with tarragon would do. Henry ate his cautiously, like a royal taster in search of poisonous taints. Once or twice the fork in his right hand clanged against his teeth. All around them people were having subdued little conversations about children, holidays, real estate, parents in care homes and villas on the Algarve. A man at the next table leaned over and said: 'I thought you were very hard on le Carré in the *Sunday Times*.' Henry, having finished the terrine, was staring at a piece of bread as if he half-expected it to go scampering off over the tablecloth. There were bygone Henrys marauding through his head, each of them promenading for a moment or so and then vanishing from sight, like models on a catwalk: Henry striding across the pavement of King's Parade; Henry in his parents' back garden at Framlingham Pigott; Henry on Southwold beach. None of them bore the slightest resemblance to any reality in which Henry the bread-inspector now participated.

Whitmore, who had finished his terrine in three predatory mouthfuls, eaten about half his seriously undercooked beef and then given up in disgust, was sitting back on his haunches with an expectant look.

'What is it you've forgiven but not forgotten?' Richard asked warily.

'The piece in the school magazine. The prefects' letter. When you said that all the fourth formers were calling me Himmler.'

'Oh that. It was a long time ago, Mark. How's the view from the dentist's chair?'

'How would I know anything about the view from the dentist's chair?'

'I thought you were a dentist.'

'Well I'm not. I work in commercial property.'

'My mistake,' Richard acknowledged. 'Did you really have Mandy Pallister on the table in the junior library?'

Whitmore looked slightly less annoyed than he had been about the view from the dentist's chair.

'It was a long time ago.'

'Everything's a long time ago.' And that was true. Everywhere you looked the signposts of a vengeful posterity were springing into place. Forty years since Henry had turned up in the school's sixth form. Thirty-seven since they had all trooped off to university, which was still called university then and not 'uni.' Thirty-four since they had barrelled on, with varying degrees of enthusiasm, into the world of work. What had Henry been like forty years ago? The answer would seem to be: a polite, ingenuous boy who wrote poems addressed to girls who were never going to go out with him, or about idealised romantic situations that had probably never existed outside a Shakespearian sonnet. The unfinished plates of beef had been taken away and Whitmore had gone off to exchange sporting chat with some people on the next table but two. Henry leant confidingly across.

'Do you think if I gave Mark Whitmore a message for Liz he'd pass it on it to her?'

'I don't see why not. Any idea where she is right now?'

'I think I heard she was living in Buckinghamshire somewhere.'

Over Henry's past life there hung the shadows of half a dozen women – maybe more – whom Henry, by his own admission, had 'never got over.' Clearly Liz Mottram, whom Richard remembered as a painfully ordinary girl with gappy teeth, was one of these.

'What do you think are the chances of her writing back?'

'I don't know' Henry said, with a kind of dreadful hang-dog defiance. 'I just want to get in touch with her.'

There were people who said, when Henry's name came up – and these were usually people who had not set eyes on him for several years – that 'something' ought to be done about him, or that 'they' – whoever they were – ought to intervene on his behalf. But this, Richard knew, would be a waste of everybody's time. It was too late to do anything about Henry, who would simply go on being himself, moving off in his one-man procession over swamps that grew deeper and less hospitable from one year to the next. Outside the refectory it was raining so hard that the windows rattled. The satyrs would be out there clacking their heels. The class of 1979 made a feeble attempt to sing 'Jerusalem', the school hymn, and then gave up. Whitmore, who still, four decades later, looked as if he intended to give the next person he saw fifty lines for insolence, came marching back from his stake-out at the adjacent table, glanced bleakly at them both and sat down again.

Richard found himself staring across the tables at some of the newer old boys and girls, who seemed less variegated than his own and earlier generations, and at the headmaster, who was looking over what were presumably the notes for the speech he was about to deliver with an air of absolutely fathomless boredom. Why on earth had he come here, Richard wondered. The answer, of course, was that you had to do something or you ended up doing nothing and turned into Henry, sitting in your cottage at Loddon glowering at the world. Just now Henry and Mark Whitmore were having a conversation about, of all things, comparative religion ('I'm delighted you believe in what you believe in,' he heard Whitmore say, not quite patronisingly, 'but I can't say it means anything to me') and he thought about Liz Mottram and her sister Cecily, now Mrs Whitmore, and various other terrible phantoms from time past. It had been a mistake to come here, he thought, a mistake to talk to Henry, a mistake to tease Mark Whitmore, and an even bigger mistake to think that any good could ever come from this kind of thing.

'Of course, the drawback to any revealed religion,' he heard Henry telling Mark Whitmore, 'is the *dogma*.'

'You know, Henry,' Mark Whitmore said, who looked almost as bored as the headmaster, 'you were exactly like this forty years ago.' But that was wrong, Richard thought. Henry had been a completely different person. Or rather, the hints of the person he was going to become were so cunningly disguised beneath the layers of charm and ingenuousness that you barely noticed they were there.

The conversation about comparative religion had ground to a halt. Further down the table someone was talking about the chances of the county council dualling the A47. It was about a quarter past ten and the menu card advertised some terrible charity game called Heads and Tails where you had to leap up and down in your seat as someone tossed a coin, followed by the headmaster's speech. Suddenly, not giving himself time to think about the decision or opportunity to regret it, he tapped Henry on the forearm of his shiny black evening suit and said: 'I can't stand this anymore. I think I'm going home.' To his surprise Henry got up too and together – not quite ostentatiously, but conscious that they were behaving badly by leaving the event before its formal closure – they walked off towards the vestibule. The rain had eased a bit and they stood watching from the doorway as they struggled into their coats.

'Did Mark Whitmore say he'd pass that message on to Liz?'

'He said if I emailed him something he'd forward it,' Henry said solemnly. What remained of his hair was sticking up on

the back of his head in an outsize tuft and he was clenching
and unclenching his fists. This drew attention to his finger-
nails, which were chewed down and curiously discoloured,
as if he had spent long hours tunnelling far underground.
Slowly they set off towards the storage hangar where Henry
had left his bike.

'Why were you so cross with Mark Whitmore?'

'Because I didn't like him when we were at school and I
don't like him now.'

'He might not have liked you. I seem to remember you
were pretty horrible to him.'

'He was pretty horrible to me.'

'He told me he'd been very ill,' Henry said, not quite
reproachfully. 'Apparently he nearly died of bacterial
pneumonia.'

There was a panic about Henry's bike, which someone
appeared to have moved from the spot in which he had concealed it, but in the end it was run to earth half-hidden under
a pile of cricket netting. The rain had stopped and the moon-
light gleaming on the surface of the playground had an oddly
sinister effect.

'Will you really email Liz Mottram?'

'She was the nicest girl I ever met,' Henry said, sounding
all of seventeen. 'If it hadn't been for all that religious stuff
. . .' Once again they were standing at the portal of a world
where only Henry could enter. What had really happened
between him and Liz Mottram – if indeed anything had happened – all those years ago was beyond reconfiguring. Like so
much concerned with Henry – Henry in his tiny cottage out
at Loddon, Henry to whom all paid employment was anath-
ema, Henry who had quarrelled with practically everyone he

had ever known – it had plunged off into the world of myth. There was no point in telling him that Liz Mottram, whatever the Circe-like qualities she might have possessed forty years ago, would be affronted by the email, or at least seriously embarrassed, and that it was better not sent.

Now that the rain had stopped it was turning colder by the minute. A muffled roar from somewhere behind them disclosed that the headmaster was leading the remaining diners in some community singing.

'Do you remember that holiday we went on in the Lake District?' Henry said. 'You and me and Olly and Katrina Watson and Katrina's French penfriend. What was her name?'

'Annick. Annick Beauregard. How could I forget it?'

But he wished Henry had not brought up the holiday in the Lake District, which was a source of shame to him. It was then that Henry had produced a leather folder in which he had bound up a typed copy of every poem he had written over the past three years and invited those present to comment. Moved by his duty to Henry, but also by his duty to poetry, Richard had spent an hour or so going through these poems, and he was still haunted by the look that had appeared on Henry's face while he had done it. But what were you supposed to do if someone who was good but not outstandingly good at writing poems asked you for your honest opinion of them? Even if you lied, or equivocated – and Richard had lied *and* equivocated – there would still be someone further down the line to say what you had not dared to say, or pronounce judgments that were a bit more unambiguously ambiguous. Still, he was ashamed of having pulled the planks from beneath Henry's feet and sent him tumbling into the river below. Or had he, when it came to it, actually sent Henry tumbling anywhere, given that he had carried on writing poems for the next thirty-five years and had probably written one that very afternoon? Henry had both hands on the bike now: one on the left handlebar, the other on the seat. He looked grim and preoccupied, absorbed by the prospect of a journey back to Loddon in his evening suit.

'Give my love to Liz Mottram,' Richard said, as a joke.

'I will,' Henry said, with apparent seriousness. He swung one leg over the frame, nearly over-balanced, but managed to regain his equilibrium and went cycling precariously off over the empty playground and out into the darkness of the cathedral close, confident as ever of the rightness of his cause, certain that the satyrs who lurked out there on civilisation's storm-crossed margin, could not drag him down.

OUT WROXHAM WAY

H ERE IN THE latish summer sun, an hour after dawn, the farm had been difficult to find. Even now, turning up a dirt track where ancient cigarette packets had been trodden into the surface of the rain-starved earth, they were not sure they had come to the right place. Something brown and anguished came streaking out of the thicket hedge on one side and disappeared into the field on the other, and Celia gave a little shriek - not the shriek of a girl who is genuinely distressed by the sight of a rat in transit, but the shriek of an actor responding to a cue. Beyond the hedge there were still strands of mist hanging over the strawberry fields, and this, together with the screeching of the gulls, gave the backdrop a mystical and at the same time faintly melancholic air, as if a gang of characters in a Thomas Hardy novel would be waiting around the corner, exclaiming over the corpse of an abandoned baby. But there were no Hardy-esque peasants and no abandoned babies, only a wide, circular stretch of gravel beyond which three or four farm buildings uneasily debouched, a few badly parked cars and several knots of aspiring fruit-pickers - too variegated and generationally distinct to be called a crowd - queueing at the farmhouse's wicker gate.

'People get up early here,' Neil said, irked at the prospect of coming several miles over the Norfolk back-roads only to find himself surplus to requirements.

Danny, counting them on his fingers and reaching a total of twenty-seven, was reassured to find all the known categories of part-time agricultural labour represented: farm-hands' wives with packets of sandwiches in sensible skirts and Wellington boots; cunning old men in moleskin trousers who looked as if they had spent the previous night in the hedge; lairy kids from the Hoveton estates; a few middle-class Norwich teenagers like Celia, Neil and himself, whose mothers had been prepared to rise at 6 a.m. and ferry them out into the countryside.

'Well, this is exciting,' Celia said, sinking to her haunches so that a shaft of sunlight caught on her bare knees and grotesquely irradiated them, like a couple of shiny soup-plates. Danny ignored her, still wondering why someone like Celia – Celia Carrington-Maule, to allow this paragon of womanhood her full name – should be squatting on the forecourt of Sharred's Farm while the lairy kids from Hoveton gawped at her legs and the old men in moleskin trousers spat fragments of tobacco over the wet grass. She was a tall, thin, strikingly self-possessed girl who went to the Norwich High School and whose mother had once caused a sensation by writing an article in the *Eastern Daily Press* about the sexual health of the young.

'Are you all right, Cee?' Neil asked, supposing that as his mother had given Celia a lift he was somehow responsible for her welfare, and Celia, gently inclining her head, rose up off her haunches in a single, graceful movement, so that Danny was reminded once again of a nature documentary he had once seen in which some rare gazelle had appeared momentarily on the forest's edge before disappearing into the cool, fronded shadow beyond.

Watching her an hour before, stashing her bicycle on the asphalt path beside the Thompsons' lean-to garage, he had been struck by the prodigious sense of incongruity, an absolute disjunction of character and environment. Kindly Mrs Thompson, goading the family car out into Christchurch Road in a series of judders, had noticed it too. 'Gracious, Celia,' she had said, eyeing the combination of satin shorts, cheesecloth smock and strappy sandals Celia had thought suitable for a day in the strawberry fields – the boys were wearing old jeans and rugby shirts – 'Are you going to a party?' Getting no answer – Celia was staring out of the window at Christchurch Road as if she had never seen it before and wondered what function it served – she went on: 'Now, where am I taking you? Out Wroxham way, is it?'

Fifty-five minutes later, Celia had exactly the same expression on her face: grave, imperturbable, yet full of dreamy content. As, not bothering to answer Neil's question, she stalked off towards the wicker gate to see what was going on, Danny tried to remember all the things he knew, or had been told, or had heard rumours about her in the two years of their desultory semi-acquaintance. They included the fact that she intended to go to Balliol College, Oxford, to read classics, that she and a band of meek-eyed acolytes had got to the regional final of the *Observer*-Mace debating competition, that she had once, in her parents' absence, held a party to which the police had been called on three separate occasions, and that she was supposed, on the last day of the preceding summer term, to have stripped down to her underwear to dance to the Norwich High School sixth-form common room record player. It was about ten past seven now and the pickers were growing impatient. In the distance, beyond the farm buildings, the last striations of mist were rolling away across the fields.

'Christ, the airs that girl gives herself,' Neil said, with what was meant to be bitter disparagement, but came out sounding half-admiring.

'Why on earth did you ask her?'

'I didn't. She rang up last night and said she'd heard we were going. Someone must have told her. I can't think why she wants to come. It's not as if she needs the money.'

In an age when most seventeen-year-olds got by on paper-rounds and Saturday jobs, a single week of Celia's allowance was once supposed to have paid for a three-course meal for four persons at Captain America's Hamburger Heaven.

'Do you think she's ever picked fruit in her life before?'

But what Neil had begun to say in reply was extinguished by a sudden shift in the crowd's alignment. All at once, in the manner of a curtain being raised above the opening of a musical comedy, several things happened. A woman with bare, mottled arms in a print frock arrived as if from nowhere and began to fling handfuls of grain from a bag that dangled at her waist in the direction of half a dozen or so stricken-looking hens that cowered on the farmyard's edge; a miniature steam engine emerged from one of the outbuildings with a small boy nervously astride its central section and came trundling towards them; and a white-haired old man appeared at the wicker gate, and in the accent of what even here in 1977 sounded like that of a stage peasant, began to issue instructions.

'There's twenty acres here. We aim to get them picked over by nightfall. Fifty pence a basket is what we pay. No more, no less. Picking for jam it is, so don't leave no stalks. Overseer find a stalk he'll run you ragged and no mistake. Now, howd you hard young feller,' – this was to one or two of the lairy

191

kids, who were making a dash for the pile of baskets – 'I ain't finished. There's a tap over there by the barn, ladies' lavatory round the side.'

The pickers looked on impassively. They had heard all this before, knew about the stalks and the ladies' lavatory. To have shown any interest would have been a betrayal of some elemental principle. The sun was properly up now and the gulls had flown off to Cromer and Winterton. In the march across to the strawberry fields he fell in alongside Celia, so close that their shoulders bumped together, and was shocked to find that she was a good inch taller than himself.

'How's Giles?' he asked, managing to remember the name of an elder brother with whom he had been on nodding terms at school, now vanished into the world of work or higher education.

'*Giles?*' Celia said, as if she had never heard the name before or, alternatively, knew a dozen Gileses, all of them so sharply defined and individuated that it was foolish of him not to specify which one. 'I think he's in Cornwall or somewhere.'

The Carrington-Maules were famous for their exotic holidays. Celia's younger brother, who had some fanciful name like Merlin or Ptolemy, had turned up at school last autumn with a FORD/DOLE IN '76 Republican lapel badge.

They were at the first of the strawberry fields now: long, neat rows of baked earth and greeny-red tracery spreading over the hill. Some of the pickers were already hard at work.

'You must tell me what I have to do,' Celia said affably, like Marie-Antoinette being asked to butter a slice of bread.

There were a number of ways of picking strawberries. The

farm-labourers' wives liked to squat on three-legged stools planted in the centre of the rows. The cunning old men preferred to hover above the plants, arthritic fingers at the ready. The lairy kids went foraging up and down the field, seizing whatever fruit lay to hand. Over the years Danny and Neil had patented a kind of sideways crouch, occasionally varied by lying full-length on the ground. Celia, having monitored these contending styles, sank bank on her splendid haunches.

'Sarah-Jane Chevenix told me all about *you*,' she said, addressing herself to Danny.

'No she didn't,' Danny said, who was determined not to take any nonsense. 'I haven't spoken to her more than twice in my life.'

'Don't think I don't know about your little excursion to – Holkham, wasn't it?'

The really awful thing about girls like Celia, Danny thought, as the first of the strawberries yielded to his touch, was not that they were spoiled, and capricious, and over-sophisticated, but that they had managed to convert these drawbacks into a viable currency. Nobody had ever dared tell them how objectionable they were and so they got away with it. You were better off with some mousy drudge who spent all her free periods in Norwich Central Library and whose bedroom shelves were lined with porcelain animal ornaments. At the same time there was a school of thought that maintained that, deep down, all the spoiled and capricious and over-sophisticated girls were just as flummoxed and subject to distress as anyone else, if not more so. As for the practical consequences of having one of these gorgons close to hand, there was no doubt that Celia's arrival had put a damper on the proceedings. Without her they would have talked about music, or other girls, or Neil's bean-counting father's attempts to make him study Chartered Accountancy. Now there was nothing to say.

As was the way of these things, they ate strawberries steadily for fifteen minutes, and then set to work. The sun was still shining brightly, but from time to time little flickers of wind dragged in from the coast sent dust scurrying away over the dried-up topsoil and towards the tall hedge that separated the strawberry fields from the rest of the farm. There were pigs quartered somewhere in the middle distance and their bitter cries came down on the breeze. Any moment now, Danny felt, Arabella Fawley would appear from one of the out-houses, knife in hand, and set off up the hill to cut their throats. Dark blood oozing over the grass; entrails flung into the boiling pan; corpses hung lengthways over the block. He opened his eyes to find that there was no Arabella and her cruel knives, no slaughtered pigs and no pale Victorian dawn, just the lines of fruit-pickers moving slowly on up the hill, the scorching sun and the sight of Celia Carrington-Maule licking strawberry juice off her chin with what would have been a come-hither look had it not also harboured the threat of disdain. The old man with the white hair marched up and down the rows at a surprisingly rapid pace, sometimes stopping to order back people who had left fruit unpicked. In this way what seemed to be enormous stretches of time passed. By eleven o'clock Danny and Neil had filled four punnets each and earned £2, while Celia, Danny noticed, was still struggling to fill her second and had earned 50p. It was then that the trouble started.

'Actually,' Celia said, with much less *sangfroid* than she

had brought to any of her previous utterances, 'I don't feel very well.'

They were polite boys, used to social occasions on which girls complained that they weren't feeling very well, and so they stopped picking strawberries and sat there for a moment, red-stained fingers poised in mid-air, waiting to see what would happen next.

'What's the matter?' Danny asked.

'I'm just not feeling terribly well,' Celia said again and left it at that. Her thin and slightly sea-horse-shaped face was paler than usual and she was taking in little gulps of air, which made the membranes in her throat quiver.

'Perhaps you ought to go and sit down in the shade,' Neil suggested, with what Danny had to admit was a far greater solicitude than he could ever have managed himself.

Celia ignored him. However ill she might have been, she was still capable of cutting wounded stragglers out of the herd. 'Would you be very kind,' she said to Danny in a strange, formal way as if they had never met each other before or, worse, he had just been found guilty of insulting her in some indefinable way, 'and go and telephone my mother and tell her I'm ill.'

'I can't very well go and phone your mother if I don't know what's wrong with you.'

Neil scooped up a palm-full of strawberries and dropped them in the basket: this problem was Danny's to deal with.

'If you must know,' Celia said, 'I think I'm going to be sick.' She sat back on her haunches, looking unspeakably forlorn, took a pencil out of her purse, wrote the number on a tiny square of paper and pressed it into his hand. 'Tell her that.'

There was no gainsaying this. Nobody - a cabinet minister, a Cinque Port Warden, the Archbishop of Canterbury - could have denied this request, and he knew better than to try. Obediently, and yet instantly cast down by the ordeal that he knew lay ahead, he made his way down the rows to the back door of the farmhouse. Here, by the grace of God there was a pay phone stuck on the badly-plastered wall, scrawled over with obscene graffiti about a girl called Hazel Ringwood, who lived at 16 Railway Cottages, Hoveton and whose phone number was several times reproduced. For a terrible moment he thought about ringing 16 Railway Cottages and seeing whether Hazel Ringwood would indeed do all the things she was advertised as enjoying. Then sanity reclaimed him and he jammed a two-pence piece in the slot. Usually if you telephoned people in their homes there was an interval of three or four rings in which you could work out what you were going to say. If you were phoning a girl you might even have written down what you were going to say on a piece of paper in advance. Frighteningly, Celia's number answered on the very first buzz.

'This is Patricia Carrington-Maule.' He had once seen Celia's mother prowling the margins of a school concert. Bony, angular and even taller than her daughter, she looked like a preying mantis bearing down on a nest of unsuspecting caterpillars.

He thought he knew how to talk to girls' mothers on the phone. You kept it terse, courteous but non-committal.

'My name is Daniel Woodrow, Mrs Carrington-Maule. I'm calling on behalf of Celia. She says she's not feeling very well.'

There was a noise of what sounded like avant-garde

electronic music mixed with the smash of crockery in the background. Mrs Carrington-Maule's reedy voice cut through this sound-collage with startling force.

'Is it her asthma again?'

'I don't think so. She said she was feeling sick.'

The avant-garde electronic music and crockery-smashing amalgam receded a bit. 'How sick, exactly?' Mrs Carrington-Maule wondered.

'I think she was hoping,' Danny said, inventing this suggestion on the spot as a means of expediting the business, 'I think she was hoping you'd come and fetch her.'

'I couldn't possibly do that,' said Mrs Carrington-Maule, earnestly and a bit affrontedly, as if he had just asked her to act as wing-man in a bank robbery or set up a publishing house to print the Larkinesque poetry he occasionally submitted to the school magazine. 'Look. Are you anywhere near a railway station?'

'About a mile away.'

'Well, tell her I'm very sorry, but she'll have to make her way home from there. Tell her to take a taxi back from the station if she's not feeling well enough to walk.'

There was a terrific crackling noise, as if Mrs Carrington-Maule were attacking someone who was trying to wrest the phone off her, some odd breathing sounds and then silence. Danny pressed the return button – you never knew – stowed the remaining two-pence pieces in the back pocket of his jeans and went back to the strawberry fields. Here events had taken a turn for the worse. Celia, whom he discovered awkwardly positioned on all fours, was quietly vomiting up undigested strawberries into a bramble bush.

'That gal's not herself,' one of the farm-labourer's wives

offered, looking up disapprovingly from her stool.

'Your mother says you'd better get the train home from Wroxham,' he said, aiming the words in the direction of Celia's satin-covered backside.

Even from a dozen feet away, the vomit stank to high heaven. People further down the rows were waving their hands in front of their faces and wrinkling their noses in disgust. After a bit Celia stopped being sick and fell back into a sitting position. He was disappointed to find that not all, in fact scarcely any, of her poise had deserted her. Neil handed her a handkerchief and she dabbed at her face with it.

'I *think*,' she said, phantom italics buzzing in the sultry air, 'I *think* that you'd better take me home.'

For a moment he thought about putting his foot down, of telling Celia that all she had done was to bring up some strawberries that had disagreed with her, that she was perfectly capable of making her own way back to Wroxham Station and after that into Norwich. But Celia lived by the will. Even now, however embarrassed she might have been by this temporary set-back, she was still capable of suborning everyone around her to its gravitational pull. On the other hand, as he thought about this, he suddenly became aware of the existence of a second, and even greater will that had had no difficulty in sending the first one sprawling in its wake. This seemed to occur to Neil too, who either out of malice or straightforward bewilderment – it was difficult to tell – said:

'Funny your mum not wanting to come and fetch you, Cee.'

There had been other moments in his life like this, when supposedly indestructible crags suddenly crumbled to dust before his eyes, when apparently invincible things and people disintegrated into nothingness. Even so, this one had come out of nowhere. Celia gave another gulp, looked as if she might be about to be sick again, but instead put her head in her hands and sobbed.

'That gal's upset,' the farm-labourer's wife volunteered.

'For Christ's sake,' Neil said.

They sat and looked at each other for a moment or so, as the noise of the pigs came skirling once again down the hill. During the crisis of the last ten minutes most of the pickers had moved on up the rows and they were almost alone. Then, spontaneously, Celia in the middle, still sobbing into her hands, they got to their feet and, leaving the half-full punnets at the field's edge for whoever might care to take them, began to walk back to the farmhouse. Celia was moistly saying something to Neil in an undertone that might or might not have referred to her mother, to which, Danny thought, Neil was attending with a bit more interest than such information warranted. As they came into the yard, where hundreds of strawberry punnets stood in a giant henge awaiting the delivery lorry, the breeze swept into his face, ruffled his hair and disturbed the collar of his rugby shirt. Here at last was the scent of autumn, rising off the Norfolk flat, bringing with it the memory of mist-bound playing fields and silent libraries, fog over the Wensum and the lights of the market shining through the dark, all those places where you could live your life on your own terms, far away from Celia, Mrs Carrington-Maule and even Hazel Ringwood of 16 Railway Cottages, Hoveton – all those devitalising influences, rapt and self-willed, bent on stopping him from becoming the person he was meant to be.

ACKNOWLEDGMENTS

I SHOULD LIKE to acknowledge the influence of Annie Proulx on 'CV' and Cathal Coughlan on 'Forty Years.' Many thanks are owing to early readers Rachel Hore, Nicholas Royle, David Collard and J. S. Barnes, Professor Peter Trudgill and Jen and Chris at Salt. Although many of these stories are site-specific, no reference is intended to any living person.

This book has been typeset by SALT PUBLISHING
LIMITED using Neacademia, a font designed by Sergei
Egorov for the Rosetta Type Foundry in the Czech
Republic. It is manufactured using Creamy 70gsm, a
Forest Stewardship Council™ certified paper from Stora
Enso's Anjala Mill in Finland. It was printed and bound
by Clays Limited in Bungay, Suffolk, Great Britain.

LONDON
GREAT BRITAIN
MMXXII